THE CASE OF THE MISSING CHEESE

A GROVE STREET MYSTERY

For Arcadia

Copyright © 2023 Lisa Mitchell.

All rights reserved. No part of this publication may be reproduced, distributed, or transmitted in any form or by any means, including photocopying, recording, or other electronic or mechanical methods, without the prior written permission of the publisher, except as permitted by U.S. copyright law.

ISBN (paperback): 979-8-9873702-2-3

This is a work of fiction. Any references to events, people, or places are used fictitiously. Names, characters, and places are products of the author's imagination.

Library of Congress Control Number: 2023914202

Cover Design & Illustrations:
Caitlin B. Alexander

Interior Book Design:
Alex Smoller

Culture & Language Consultants:
Juan Barbecho
Maria Estefani Chinchilla Lemus
Eva Versaci

First edition, 2023.

SparkBright Kids, Mount Kisco, NY
SparkBrightKids.com

SPARKBRIGHT
KIDS

CONTENTS

1. Mount Brighton 1
2. The Grove Street Detective Agency. 7
3. Lemonade and Cheese. 30
4. The Mount Brighton Carnival. 55
5. Conversations 80
6. Disappearing Cheese. 96
7. Suspect Number One: Señorita Flores 107
8. Suspect Number Two: Declan 120
9. Suspect Number Three: The Zmetila 134
10. Exoneration. 146
11. Suspect Number Four: Skyler 156
12. Case Closed. 164

Epilogue 186

1
MOUNT BRIGHTON

Three people lived at number One Grove Street. Three people, two dogs, and probably five hundred spiders. Skyler Starshine, one of the three people, did not like to think about the five hundred spiders, because the spiders lived in the basement, and the basement was the second scariest place on earth. Skyler was the only kid in the house, which was a little bit special and a little bit lonely, but mostly it was just normal because that was how it had always been. Spiders and basements were not the only things that scared Skyler. Ever since she started third grade, lots of things seemed more frightening. "Anxiety," her mom called it. "Just part of growing up," her dad said. *I hope it doesn't last forever*, Skyler thought.

Mount Brighton Elementary School was not your typical elementary school, because the kids there learned in two languages. Most schools only come in one language, and in the state of New York in the United States of America on the planet Earth, that language was usually English. But not at MBES! At MBES the kids got school in English *and* Spanish, because some Mount Brighton families spoke English at home (like Skyler's), some spoke Spanish (like Juan's), and the luckiest ducks of all, some families spoke both (like Izzy's). Maybe other Mount Brighton families didn't speak English *or* Spanish and felt a little bit left out. That made Skyler sad when she thought about it.

Whether they spoke English or Spanish at home, the MBES kids all had something in common—they were learning to be fluent in another language. *Fluency* is when you have all the words you need to say what you mean. Another thing you should know about Skyler: words were her superpower.

One of the best things about MBES was that every kid got two teachers. Señorita Flores was Skyler's Spanish days teacher, and Mr. Campbell was her English days teacher. Every other day, the kids switched rooms, ping-ponging between English and Spanish. Sometimes it was tricky to remember which room to go to, but other than that, having two teachers was awesome. Mr. Campbell loved hiking and spending time outside, so the class visited the school garden a lot. The kids planted fruits and vegetables and then harvested them for the food pantry, which gave it out to families in need. Garden days were the best days.

Number One Grove Street, with its humans, dogs, and spiders, was nestled at the end of a quiet, dead-end street in the little town. Well, kind of little. Mount Brighton's motto was "The Big Small Town." Mount Brighton didn't take up very much space, which made it small. Skyler could walk to school and to the diner and also to the movie theater and train station (the train went into New York City, which was so big, it might actually have been humongous). But there were also a bunch of people and tons of things to do, so it felt big. A carnival even came to town every September, and people from the other towns (where the schools only came in English) would ride the roller coaster and eat cotton candy. Skyler could walk to the carnival *and* order her cotton candy en español.

There is one more thing to know about Skyler, her five hundred spiders, and the residents of

Mount Brighton. On a sunny September day after the Mount Brighton carnival, a very special cheese vanished into thin air. And that is where our mystery begins: with Skyler, the one and only kid at One Grove Street, and a town full of suspects.

2

THE GROVE STREET DETECTIVE AGENCY

Skyler kicked the red rubber ball against the bricks of Mount Brighton Elementary School, which returned it to her feet with a *sproing*.

"Tomorrow, let's have a lemonade stand," Izzy said, "and on Sunday, we can walk to the carnival."

Skyler smiled. She loved making weekend plans without consulting her parents.

"I'll bring brownies," Juan said. "My mom can

make them in the morning, and we can sell them for one dollar each. We'll make a fortune!"

Juan thought about all the corn dogs, ride tickets, and carnival games he could spend his lemonade loot on.

"I'll make the lemonade," Izzy declared. "Skyler, what will you bring?"

In the time it took the brick wall to return the rubber ball, Skyler blurted out the first idea that popped into her head: "Enchanted pineapple juice muddled under a blue moon!" Juan scratched his head and gave Skyler a look that said *I don't know if that's real or not.*

"Whoa!" Izzy said. "Are you sure you can get that?"

"Get it?" Skyler asked. "I'm going to make it! Good thing there's a blue moon tonight! All I need is a pineapple to muddle." She also needed a spell to cast, but she didn't tell her friends that. She had plenty of time to come up with a spell. How hard could it be?

"Muddle?" asked Juan, still processing the enchanted and moon parts.

"That's when you smash fruit up with a stick," Skyler retorted smugly.

Trilllll. The shiny whistle that hung around Mr. Campbell's neck interrupted the kids and told them recess was over. They shuffled into a line and proceeded through the big, old doors of the school, each locked in a daydream. Juan wondered what it was like to go to school before computers. Izzy wondered if Señorita Flores always clipped her hair back with a pretty yellow-rose barrette because her last name meant "flowers," or if it was just a coincidence. Skyler wondered where she would find a spell for enchanted pineapple juice muddled under a blue moon.

+ + + + +

At three o'clock the rusty red dismissal bell rang, as it had daily for generations. Kids poured out of the worn doors, gathering near the playground. Skyler pulled a yellow notepad out of her pocket so that she and Izzy could compare Mystery Mayhem notes while they waited for their friends.

The Mystery Mayhem game captivated everyone at the school, even some teachers. To play the game, teams searched for clues with a beacon that beeped and glowed when a team member was near an official Mystery Mayhem clue. Skyler's mom said it used the same technology as the GPS map on her phone. She also said that it was incredibly annoying. Right now, the Grove Street Detective

Agency—that was Skyler, Izzy, and Juan's team—was in the lead. As Skyler and Izzy tried to make sense of the latest Mystery Mayhem hint, Lucia approached with Phoebe, whose tiara was a bit more crooked than it was on the morning walk to school.

"How's the case going?" Lucia asked.

"Are you going to solve it in time?" Phoebe added.

"I hope so," Skyler said. She chewed her pencil as she thought. The Grove Street Detective Agency were the best in town, but another team in Springbrook, one town over, was close behind. If Skyler, Izzy, and Juan could solve this case by next Friday, though, they would be the local champions—and the first team in Mount Brighton ever to win. Time was running out, and they were neck and neck with the Springbrook Sleuths. "We still need to find two more clues, and we only have a week left. It'll be tough, but we might be able to pull it off."

"There's no school next Friday—it's Superintendents' Conference Day! That gives you a little extra time," Phoebe said.

"But what the heck does this hint mean?" Izzy puzzled. She squinted at the Mystery Mayhem hint Skyler had scribbled in her notepad and read aloud, "Don't be sold a story."

Just then, Juan jogged past the group, high-fiving his friends on his way to Bus Number Four. Even though he lived on Grove Street, he took the bus to the after-school program across town where he learned robotics while his parents were at work. His aunt would pick him up at five o'clock, and he'd return to Grove Street for homework, dinner, and of course, Mystery Mayhem.

"Bye, guys!" Juan yelled. "Izzy, Skyler—pay attention to the beacon when you get to our street! I really do think it's somewhere in *his* yard."

Skyler shivered. She hated thinking about the mean old man on the corner. In fact, she had vowed never to go into his yard, not ever again. Skyler fidgeted with the Mystery Mayhem beacon—a hexagonal device that hung around her neck, and the key to the whole game.

"If it's in his yard, you babies don't stand a chance," a voice sneered from behind. It was Javier, Juan's fifth-grade cousin who lived around the corner on Main Street. "Zmetila!" he barked at Skyler, making her jump.

"Don't you dare!" Skyler yelled, shuddering. She didn't even know what that word meant, but the mean old man sure liked screaming it at her. Which was one of the reasons for her vow.

Suddenly, a blond streak whizzed by.

"Wait up, Juan!" Declan cried. Declan lived way across town, but his parents really liked MBES, so he had a long bus ride to school. Because MBES had classes in two languages, families could decide if they wanted their kids to go there or not. Declan always complained about Spanish days—learning in two languages was tough—but he loved his teachers and friends and wouldn't change it for the world.

Declan hunched over and rubbed his side halfway to the bus. His tummy was bothering him that day because Señorita Flores's class had earned an ice cream party for only speaking in español for one whole day. He was lactose intolerant, which meant things like milk, cheese, and ice cream gave him a stomachache, but he couldn't resist.

As the buses rolled onto the street, the pack of kids left the schoolyard. When they reached the neighborhood, Phoebe, a second grader, peeled off from the group and ran down Pine Street toward her house, her tutu flouncing as she went.

"See you tomorrow!" she squealed. Like Skyler, Phoebe spoke English at home and learned Spanish at school. And also like Skyler, Phoebe was an only child. But those were about the only things they had in common. Phoebe was what Skyler called a "surprise friend." Phoebe liked dresses, and princesses, and tea parties, and unicorns. Skyler liked pants, and dinosaurs, and mud kitchens, and also unicorns. Phoebe loved dancing. She went to dance class four days a week and even did dance competitions and parades! Skyler liked karate and had just earned her purple belt. Even though they were very, very different, they were good friends, which was the best kind of surprise.

Skyler, Izzy, and Lucia waved goodbye and continued up the hill toward home.

"Let's cross," Skyler suggested as they approached Grove Street. She wanted to stay as far away from the house on the corner as possible. Luckily, Lucia lived on the other side of the street, so there was a good excuse for crossing. As the kids headed down the block, they saw Lucia's abuela waiting on the sidewalk.

"¡Hola, mija!" she said, waving to her granddaughter. Lucia lived with her mom and abuela in the yellow house across from Izzy. Lucia didn't speak English in kindergarten, but now she did. Her abuela spoke mostly Spanish but had learned a good bit of English. She volunteered at the library, so Lucia got to go to all the fun library events.

"¿Cómo te fué en la escuela?" her abuela asked, bouncing the baby on her shoulder.

"¡Excelente!" Lucia replied. She reached into her bag and proudly produced a beautiful painting of the Mount Brighton carnival.

"Que arte tan hermoso," her grandmother crooned.

With a wave, the remaining two girls headed toward Izzy's house. The Mystery Mayhem beacon glowed and beeped as they crossed the street again. Izzy gave Skyler a worried look.

"I think Juan's right," Izzy said. She stared at the beacon that hung around Skyler's neck. "Let's check again tonight after dinner."

"Hi, girls!" Izzy's mom interrupted from the porch. Izzy's mom spoke Spanish and English, but her dad only spoke English. Even though her mom *and* her grandma *and* her aunts all spoke

Spanish, Izzy didn't really start learning it until she started school at MBES. They used to only speak English at home, but ever since Izzy started school, her mom has been insisting on a little Spanish every day. Skyler's mom was surprised to learn that Izzy's mom spoke Spanish. "I'm so jealous," she remembered her mother saying. "I wish I could understand the Spanish homework."

"See you tonight," Izzy said. "We'll figure it out."

"That's *if* you finish your homework and do your chores, Iz. That cage is starting to stink!" Izzy's mom said.

"Cage?" Skyler asked.

"It's a surprise!" Izzy squealed. "I'll show you this weekend after I get everything set up."

And then it was just Skyler, one girl, all alone on Grove Street. She ran the rest of the way home, partly because she was hungry, but mostly because she didn't like being anywhere near the old man's house without her friends.

+ + + + +

At six-thirty, the three members of the Grove Street Detective Agency assembled halfway down the block. Juan's mom called out, "¡Ven a casa antes de que oscurezca!"

"But Mo-om," Juan called back, "sunset is so early!" Juan's mom knew what he meant even though neither of his parents spoke English. She gave him a look that said *I mean it*. "Está bien," Juan huffed.

The Grove Street Detective Agency walked toward the end of the street. Every few steps, the Mystery Mayhem beacon glowed brighter and brighter. The beeps grew faster and louder. They had been working on this mystery, the Case of the Lonely Heart, for two months and had collected almost all the clues. Only two remained, and if they found them, they'd crack the case and become the regional champions! No one from Mount Brighton had ever won, and the Grove Street Detective Agency was determined.

"I'm telling you, it has *got* to be in his yard," Juan said. He pointed a thumb at the dark house on the corner. Just glancing at it gave Skyler a pit in her stomach.

The kids called the old man who lived there the Zmetila, because they didn't know anything about him, not even his name, although they guessed he was about 170 years old. He didn't speak English or Spanish. They had only heard him say a few things in a language none of them knew, usually when he yelled at squirrels. That was where his nickname came from. He loved to scream "Zmetila!" at the squirrels. Whenever the Grove Street kids walked past the Zmetila's house, like they did that evening, Skyler took a deep breath in through her nose. The house always smelled a little like meatball sauce. Delicious, delicious meatball sauce from a scary, scary house.

Once, Javier and Declan thought it would be funny to toilet-paper the Zmetila's yard. They were just about finished when the Zmetila saw them and started yelling "Zmetila! Zmetila!" out the window. It was hilarious watching them jump out of their skin and tear down the street. Skyler stopped laughing, however, when she saw the old man's face as he began removing the toilet paper from the rose bushes his wife used to care for before she stopped coming outside as much. The Zmetila locked eyes with her, his stare silently accusing her of conspiring with the boys.

Skyler had been terrified of the old man ever since that day, but her fear grew stronger when the kids started playing Mystery Mayhem. Early in the summer, when they first signed up for the game and received their homing beacon, they ran through the neighborhood, handing out flyers. Mystery Mayhem was a sensation that swept the country, and the more people who played, the more fun it was. The flyers invited neighbors to sign up and receive a clue card, which they were responsible for attaching to an object and hiding somewhere in the community.

To play, you needed a team of friends to create a detective agency. Each agency received a homing beacon in the mail, which glowed and beeped when it was close to a Mystery Mayhem clue. When a detective agency found a clue, the next one unlocked and a message appeared on the beacon with hints as to where it might be. *But*, if another detective agency got to the clue first, a red fish appeared on the screen and rerouted the team to another clue, which meant all that time had been wasted. The dreaded Red Herring.

The game was sort of like a cross between a scavenger hunt and geocaching—an activity Mr. Campbell had told them about where people hide real treasures in the woods so that players can track them down with their phones. When a detective agency collected all five clues, they cracked the case. The Grove Street Detective Agency had been working on the Case of the Lonely Heart for two months. If they found the last two clues and solved the case by next Friday, they would win the game!

"Remember the Mystery Mayhem code," Skyler said to her friends. She put one hand on her heart and recited,

"You need witnesses, evidence, and motives to solve,
a mystery that will always evolve.
New detectives and suspects join by the day,
but teamwork and thinking will show you the way.
Open your heart and sharpen your mind,
think fast, crack the case, but always be kind.
Be brave, take a risk, you might find a friend.
Love and community win in the end."

"And?" asked Izzy, wondering what the

Mystery Mayhem code had to do with searching the Zmetila's yard.

"There can't be a clue in that yard," Skyler said. "That old man would have never signed up for a Mystery Mayhem clue. He has no motive!"

"Maybe someone else hid the clue in his yard," Juan offered.

"That's against the rules," Skyler retorted. She ignored the fact that Juan could be right because she was *not* going to go into that yard, not ever again. "Clues have to be hidden on public property, like parks and stuff. You're only allowed to hide them on private property if you own it."

"*And* if you're OK with a bunch of kids running through your yard," Izzy chimed in, "which the Zmetila definitely is *not*."

"I think Skyler's just scared cause of what happened," Juan said.

Skyler shuddered. "I'm not scared," she lied. She scrunched her eyes and stared at the ground, recalling the time she ran into the Zmetila's yard with a handful of Mystery Mayhem flyers. It was just before the end of last school year, and she had finally mustered up the guts to knock on his door after the toilet paper incident. She had prepared a speech saying she thought it was awful what the boys did, but she didn't have anything to do with it. She would then hand him a flyer and invite him to sign up to hide a clue.

She had taken a deep breath and ran up his gravel path holding a stack of flyers. But before she reached the door, she tripped and fell, scattering flyers all over the yard and skinning her knees badly. She dusted herself off, fighting back tears from the pain while pulling little pebbles out of her scratched-up knees. Suddenly, the front door flew open. She felt a sense of relief, knowing a grown-up was there to help, but the old man barked at her using words she didn't understand.

He shook and shouted, and even though she couldn't understand anything he said, Skyler felt like she was in the biggest trouble of her life. She tried to explain that it was an accident, that she wasn't trying to ruin his garden like Javier and Declan, but they didn't understand each other. In fact, he yelled so much that his frail wife, who no longer came outside very often, came to the door and said something to make him stop. She looked at Skyler with kind, tired eyes, but it was too late. Skyler burst into tears and ran home. She promised to never, ever go back ever again.

"This thing must be busted," she said, tapping the beacon just a little too hard. "There's no way it's at his house. Let's check the empty one again."

Sometimes the Grove Street kids played in the backyard of the empty house across from the Zmetila, even though they knew they shouldn't. There were lots of rumors about what happened to the people who used to live in the house, but Skyler's mom said that they had just moved to Cincinnati.

"Not tonight, Skyler," Juan said. "I told my mom I'd be home before dark, and besides, we know there's nothing back there. The beacon doesn't go off near that house."

"OK," Skyler said. She tried not to look as disappointed as she felt. It was the worst feeling—because it was at herself, for being scared. "I guess that's all for tonight, then."

"This is going to be the best weekend ever!" Izzy said to brighten the mood. "Eleven o'clock at my house tomorrow for the lemonade stand and then the carnival on Sunday!"

"Only two more days!" Juan cried. He jabbed his fist in the air.

Yes, there were two more days until the carnival. But little did the kids know, there were also only two days until the real mystery began.

3

LEMONADE AND CHEESE

The next morning, Skyler woke up excited for the lemonade stand. "You said you'd bring *what?*" asked Skyler's mom, in a way that meant it wasn't really a question. She sighed one of her exasperated sighs.

"Don't worry, Mom. We just need a pineapple to muddle," Skyler said.

"But it's not even pineapple season," Skyler's

mom said, as if it was ever pineapple season in New York.

Skyler made her eyes say *this is really important to me,* so her mom got the car keys and they drove to the store. *Sometimes not using words is more effective*, Skyler thought.

Unimpressed by the pineapple prices, her mom led them to the juice aisle, where Skyler picked a pineapple-mango blend that said *organic* on the front. She scribbled *organic* in her yellow notepad, which said *Words, Ideas, and Mysteries* on the cover.

"Hang on. I want to pick up some cheese while we're here," her mom said.

Skyler took short steps on her tiptoes so that her sneakers squeaked on the shiny linoleum floor as they walked past the deli counter to the cheese case. There were so many types of cheese!

Skyler's parents were hosting a drinks-and-snacks party that night, so her mom picked out five types of fancy cheese: aged Gouda, Gruyère, Brie, Gorgonzola, and Manchego. Manchego was Skyler's favorite cheese in the world. Gorgonzola was her least favorite cheese in the world. It smelled like a rotten sock that a pig had taken a nap on. She tried to hide it in the bottom of the cart, but her mom still bought it. Skyler could tell because she could smell it all the way from the trunk the whole ride home.

+ + + + +

When they returned from the store, Skyler knew she only had a few minutes to get ready for the lemonade stand. The blue moon was last night (or was it last week or last year?), and because her mom bought organic juice in a carton, she couldn't even muddle it. Her plans were falling apart! She decided that if she poured it into a pitcher under something blue, that was the next best thing.

"Come on, Skyler, you're going to be late to the lemonade stand," her mom called from the living room. "Let's go."

Skyler heard her mom toss the keys into her purse and knew she had only moments to cast the spell. Her eyes darted frantically around the kitchen, looking for anything blue. The cheese! She reached for the Gorgonzola, which her mom had left under a glass dome to ripen. Gorgonzola is a kind of blue cheese, which gets its name from the blue mold that grows all over it. *Blech. Why would anyone eat mold?* Skyler thought.

She carefully lifted the glass dome off the wooden cutting board and was immediately whacked by the pungent aroma of old socks and barnyard. Skyler held her breath and raised the cheese as high above her head as her arm would allow. It squished in her hand, and she wondered if the smell would ever come off. With her other hand, she poured the pineapple-mango juice into a pitcher (so that it looked homemade) and recited a spell that she made up on the spot.

"Pineapple juice, so nice and sweet
Bring fortune to the kids of Grove Street.
And one more thing to make me cheer:
Make the stinky cheese disappear!"

"Pee-ew!" her mom exclaimed as she entered the kitchen, wafting the air in front of her nose. "What is that smell?"

"It's the cheese, Mom! It's awful!" Skyler stuck out her tongue and made a retching sound.

"That is intense, even for my taste," Skyler's mom said. "And why are you holding it? Never mind. Put it in a baggie, and we'll bring it to

Izzy's house. Let's get it out of here!"

Skyler packed the cheese in three zip-top bags to try to contain the smell. Then she grabbed the pitcher and they headed out. As they passed the dark house on the corner, the Mystery Mayhem beacon began to glow and sound.

"That's odd," Skyler's mom said.

"I think it needs new batteries or something," Skyler said dismissively. She did not want to draw any unnecessary attention to the Zmetila's house.

When they arrived, Izzy and Juan had already moved Izzy's craft table to the sidewalk in front of her house. Juan carried a toy cash register, the kind you play make-believe with in kindergarten, and set it carefully in the middle of the table. Izzy wrote the menu in chalk on the plain side of the big blue mailbox on the sidewalk—the kind the post office used to collect outgoing mail.

"Do you think it's OK to write on this?" Izzy asked no one in particular.

"It's probably illegal," Skyler said. "But I doubt they'll arrest a bunch of third graders for vandalism with sidewalk chalk."

Izzy looked confused.

"Vandalism?" Juan asked for her.

"It's when you wreck something that isn't yours," Skyler replied.

"Javier did vandalism on my CharmBots cards," Juan muttered, kicking a pebble with the side of his shoe.

In her best handwriting, Izzy wrote:

For Sale

Lemonade: $1

Brownies: $1

Pineapple Juice: $3

Just then, a sleek silver car with dark windows

rolled past. It slowed to a stop, and the driver rolled down the window. Too much cologne seeped out from the car as the driver looked down his nose and over his sunglasses at the kids. The man had crunchy hair, like he used too much of the gel Juan's mom combs in when he goes to church. *The crunchy-haired man*, thought the kids.

"Could you *not* do that?" the man said to Izzy in disdain. His face looked like he was smelling something bad. Noticing something was off, Izzy's mom approached.

"They're little kids making a lemonade stand. What is the problem exactly?" she asked firmly but not unkindly.

"I'm never going to sell this place," the man muttered, rolling up his window and driving down the block to park in front of the empty house. There was a "For Sale" sign in the yard.

It had been there for months, so long that the grass was tufting around it where they couldn't mow.

Juan had a bad feeling. He didn't like the way the man looked at him. Shaking it off, he asked, "Why is the pineapple juice so much more expensive?"

"Because Skyler muddled it under a blue moon! That makes it super rare and also magic. That's gotta be worth at least three bucks," Izzy replied. Then she squinted her eyes at her friend. "You did enchant it, right, Skyler?"

"Oh yeah," Skyler responded, sniffing the hand that held the stinky cheese.

"Sofia," Skyler's mom said to Izzy's mom, "we have some extra Gorgonzola—maybe you want it or could pass it along? I'd hate to see it go to waste."

Izzy's mom took the cheese and examined the multiple bags containing it.

"Sure," she said, a little taken aback by the unusual offering. "Maybe Angelo will appreciate this. He's gone through such a hard time recently, and some cheese from home might be just what the doctor ordered. Thanks!" She went inside to put the cheese in the kitchen, dodging the kids as they went back and forth, bringing brownies, lemonade, plates, and napkins out to the table.

"I'll be back in a couple of hours, Skyler. Good luck with the lemonade stand, kids!" Skyler's mom called. Then she texted the neighborhood chat on her way back home: *Attention neighbors! Lemonade stand at 431 Grove!*

"There's one more lemonade-stand worker you two need to meet," Izzy said, running inside. Skyler and Juan ran behind her. "Move it, Olivia," Izzy said to her little sister before shoving her out of the way with a hip jab. A big metal crate sat atop the old TV stand in Izzy's living room. It had a thick bed of sawdust lining the bottom. Nestled under a fake log was the cutest thing Skyler had ever seen!

"Meet Cheese, my new hamster!" Izzy removed the lid of the cage and carefully scooped up Cheese, who nibbled a kernel of corn.

"You mean *our* new hamster," Izzy's mom piped in, gesturing to three-year-old Olivia, who was now chewing on the leg of a Barbie and staring out the window at the line of grown-ups in front of the lemonade stand. "And by the smell coming from that cage, you are not taking your pet care responsibilities seriously enough."

Skyler had to agree about that. Although he was cute, Cheese's cage stunk.

Izzy's mom continued, "I put the shoebox and a garbage bag next to the fresh sawdust, Iz. Don't forget what the vet said. If you put some food and water in the shoebox, Cheese won't be scared in there. Please clean it out today."

Ignoring her mom, Izzy passed the hamster to Skyler, who couldn't believe her friend would trust her with such a special thing. He was warm and lighter than she expected, like holding a sunny cloud.

"Why did you name him Cheese?" Skyler asked, thinking maybe Cuddles or Fluffy would be a more fitting name, based on the softest thing in the world that had curled up in her cupped hands.

"Because he looks like a cheese stick, obviously! That's his full name, but we call him Cheese for short," Izzy replied. She grabbed the hamster back and held him up so that the kids could get a better look.

Skyler and Juan studied the hamster, who had

a fluffy white body, a soft brown head, two cute little brown ears, a white face, two beady black eyes, and an adorable pink nose. Neither of the kids quite understood how Cheese looked like a cheese stick, but when your friend is proud of something, you don't vandalize their pride.

"Mom and Dad said I wasn't responsible enough for a pet, but I convinced them I am. Plus, if I can show them I'm ready with Cheese, maybe we can get a dog next," Izzy said dreamily.

"Customers!" cried Juan. He gestured to the

gathering crowd on the sidewalk. The kids bolted for the door, Izzy clutching Cheese against her chest.

Izzy (and Cheese) took orders, Skyler served the customers, and Juan manned the cash register. He could figure out change in his head without a calculator or even a pencil! If words were Skyler's superpower, then numbers were Juan's. And they needed every superpower they could get! It seemed as if for every cup of lemonade poured, two more people would arrive. The whole neighborhood must have turned up. How had word spread so quickly? Had the magic spell worked? Was fortune being bestowed upon the kids of Grove Street?

During the rush, the crunchy-haired man glared at the kids as he walked from the house that was for sale back to his car, parked on the street.

"A rodent at a lemonade stand?" he barked,

rolling his eyes. "Someone should call the health department."

A group of neighbors laughed, but Izzy gave him a hard stare. The crunchy-haired man looked over his sunglasses and pointed at his own cold eyes with two fingers before turning them to point directly at Cheese. Izzy knew what that meant: he was watching them.

"Leave my hamster alone!" she cried.

The kids kept pouring drinks, serving brownies, and making change. At one point it got so busy that Izzy had to help fill the orders, too. To free up her hands, she put Cheese into the driver's seat of Olivia's Barbie car, which she left carelessly on the grass. A bunch of grown-ups took out their phones to take pictures of the hamster driving the pink convertible Corvette, and Olivia sat gleefully pushing the car around the yard.

Twenty minutes later the crowd thinned out and only one customer remained. Skyler called out, "That's the end of the lemonade! There's a little enchanted pineapple juice left, and two brownies."

"Thirty-five, thirty-six, thirty-seven," Juan said, counting the proceeds aloud while Izzy tied up the trash bag with the used cups. Suddenly, a shadow cast over the table and a chill ran down Skyler's spine. She told herself it was nothing. She *had* to get control over this fear. She took a deep breath to steady her nerves and looked up to serve the last customer. Glowering back at her was . . . the Zmetila.

"I suddenly remembered I have to pee," Juan squeaked out. Then he bolted inside. He grabbed Olivia on his way, in what he thought was a heroic act.

"I think I heard m-m-my m-m-mom call me," Izzy stammered, following Juan's lead.

Skyler swallowed. Her friends had abandoned her. Alone and face-to-face with the Zmetila, She felt her cheeks go cold and her knees turn wobbly.

"Enchanted pineapple juice?" she asked meekly, eyes cast down to the street.

"Sì," the Zmetila grunted.

Skyler was hit with a realization and barely

found the courage to say it. "Oh! You *do* speak Spanish! I mean, ¿usted habla español?" she managed softly, forcing her eyes upward. If she could tell him it was all a misunderstanding in Spanish, maybe he'd understand and the fear would start to go away.

"No," grunted the Zmetila, narrowing his eyes.

Skyler returned her gaze to the safety of the sidewalk. She did not understand. If he didn't speak Spanish, why was he responding to her with Spanish words? "Sí" means "yes" in Spanish, and "no" means, well, "no."

Her hand shook as she poured the orangey-yellowish pineapple juice into the flimsy plastic cup. It trembled as she handed the last of the enchanted juice to the Zmetila. She felt his tough, leathery skin as he took it from her, his hand bumping her own. The Zmetila's hand trembled, too, but more in an old way than a scared way. He grabbed the cup a little too hard, and Skyler gasped as a small crack appeared on the side. Sticky pineapple juice dribbled down his hand. Was he going to yell at her again?

Too afraid to tell him the juice cost three dollars, Skyler just stood there, stunned. The old man put the cup back down on the table with a little too much force. He knelt down to tie his shoe, studying the nervous child before him as he did. The Zmetila crouched awkwardly over Barbie's Corvette, slowly tightening the laces of his old leather boot but never taking his eyes off Skyler. Then he stood up, reached into his back pocket, and produced a crisp five-dollar bill from an old-fashioned money clip. He tossed the bill on top of the still-open cash register and shuffled off down the street.

After a few paces he paused, looked back, and said, "Smettila di aver paura di me. Sono solo un vecchio solitario."

He raised his cup toward Skyler as if to say "cheers" and then toward the three faces stacked on top of one another in the window. Izzy and Juan flashed nervous smiles, while Olivia, who was at the top of the stack, made her Barbie dance on her sister's hair with one hand. With the other, she waved enthusiastically. Then he continued down the street, feeling awkward and sad, despite knowing that his wife would have been proud of him for visiting the lemonade stand.

A few moments later, Juan and Izzy emerged cautiously from the house. They peered down the street to confirm the old man had gone. Then they rushed to their friend.

"Did you actually talk to him?"

"What did he say?"

"Did he pay?"

"Could you tell how old he is?"

Skyler did her best to answer the questions as quickly as they asked them. After a whirlwind interrogation, the three kids collapsed in the grass. Olivia resumed playing with the Barbie car, pushing it around the yard. Staring up at the clear blue sky, Skyler said, "Guys, he told me he didn't speak Spanish *in Spanish.*"

"That doesn't even make any sense," Izzy said.

"And you left me," Skyler managed to say. It sounded squished, which was how she felt.

Izzy and Juan exchanged a guilty look.

"Let's count the money," Juan said. They needed something to do to take their minds off the Zmetila.

+ + + + +

"Sixty-three dollars! We made sixty-three dollars!" Juan said in disbelief. "That's twenty-one dollars each! Although, maybe we should make it twenty each so we can give Olivia a three-dollar tip for helping with cleanup."

The kids agreed and Juan started doling out the cash.

"Honey, where's Cheese?" Izzy's mom called out from the porch.

Cheese! Oh no! In the flurry of customers, Izzy had put him in Barbie's Corvette and forgotten about him. She burst into tears.

"It's OK, Izzy. We'll help find him," Skyler said, patting her friend on the back. The kids frantically searched in the grass and bushes for their friend's brand-new pet hamster. Izzy's mom hugged Izzy tight with one arm and rubbed her own forehead with the other hand.

Skyler looked under the vandalized mailbox while Juan crawled under the porch. After several deep breaths, Izzy joined the search party and crawled on her hands and knees through the grass, looking for tiny footprints or hamster poo—any clues that would lead her to Cheese. And where was the Barbie car? Had Cheese driven off into the horizon?

After what seemed like an eternity, Olivia toddled over from the backyard to the front yard, swinging her Barbie by the hair. "Whatcha doing, Iz?" she asked.

"Cheese is lost!" Izzy wailed, her bottom lip trembling.

"Cheese is not lost. Cheese is having tea with the fairies!" Olivia put a comforting hand on Izzy's back and did her best to help her up. She led everyone to the backyard, where her fairy house stood proudly at the edge of the surrounding woods. Barbie's Corvette was parked out front, as if Cheese had just driven home from a hard day at the office. Izzy carefully opened the tiny door to the fairy house, crouched down, and peered inside.

There sat Cheese, with a fairy-size table in front of him. Olivia had filled the top of an acorn with water, and he was blissfully lapping it up.

"Cheese!" Izzy cried, scooping up her beloved pet and knocking the delicate fairy house over. "Cheese, Cheese, Cheese!" The kids jumped and cheered.

With Cheese safely back in his cage, the friends collapsed on the couch, relishing the air-conditioning and a moment of calm. Just then, Skyler's mom knocked on the door.

"Alright, kids," Izzy's mom said. "I think that's

just about enough excitement for one day. Skyler, your mom is here. Juan, get your things. Izzy, time for chores."

"Awww," the kids all whined in unison.

"What's with all the frowns?" Skyler's mom joked. "These don't look like the faces of kids ready to spend their lemonade money at the carnival tomorrow!"

The carnival was the best day of the year in Mount Brighton. They had six days to crack the Mystery Mayhem case and had agreed to only work on the game in the morning so that they could all enjoy an afternoon filled with rides and treats. It had been a successful Saturday and Cheese was back in his cage, safe and sound . . . at least, for now.

4

THE MOUNT BRIGHTON CARNIVAL

The next morning, Izzy and Juan tore down the street to Skyler's house. With the hours before the carnival, they hoped to crack the Mystery Mayhem case, or at least make progress. The Case of the Lonely Heart was the toughest one yet. The kids pored over their notes, trying to decipher the latest hint from Mystery Mayhem HQ.

"'Don't be sold a story,'" Juan recited. "Maybe

it's at the bookstore?" Skyler tapped her pencil against her chin, trying to remember if the beacon glowed the last time she was downtown.

"Izzy," Skyler's mom interrupted, "your mom just called. She says you need to finish your chores before you can go to the carnival. Get a move-on. We're leaving soon." Izzy's parents were always on her case about cleaning her room, unloading the dishwasher, and taking care of Cheese.

"Ugh, sorry, guys," Izzy said. "I'll be back soon. Don't leave without me."

+ + + + +

Izzy returned faster than anyone had expected, and the kids skipped off to the carnival with their lemonade fortunes in tow. Juan stashed his earnings in his CharmBots hip bag next to the sunblock his dad made him bring. The black bag featured a bright yellow MerliTron—Juan's favorite CharmBot, not because he looked cool but because his special magic power was invisibility and his special robot power was code-breaking. Izzy brought her white-cat-wearing-glitter-sunglasses purse for the express purpose of carrying her lemonade loot, and Skyler folded her money up and tucked it into her sock. When they reached the corner, the Mystery Mayhem beacon chirped and glowed.

"I'm telling you—" Juan started.

"Not today, Juan. Today is all about the carnival!" Izzy interrupted.

Skyler exhaled, relieved she didn't have to come up with another excuse to avoid the Zmetila's house.

"Yeah, we have all week, plus there is no school on Friday. Tons of time," Skyler agreed.

As they rounded the corner into town, they could hear the carnival sounds—the recorded organ music of the carousel, people screaming on the roller coaster, and the local band, Exit Four, playing on the steps of town hall.

"Race ya!" Skyler squealed to her friends. "Last one there is stinky Gorgonzola!"

Juan, Izzy, and Skyler tore off, leaving Skyler's mom behind.

"Stay together!" she called. "Meet at the fountain if you get separated! I'll be there with my book! See you at four o'clock!"

The three kids arrived at the ticket booth at precisely the same time, proving that none of them were, in fact, stinky Gorgonzola.

As the kids read the ticket sign, someone bumped Juan from behind. It was Javier.

"Hey!" Juan said, rubbing his shoulder.

"Are you babies even tall enough for the rides?" Javier asked with a sneer.

Skyler and Izzy knew that the cousins fought like siblings and left things to their friend.

"We're not babies," Juan retorted. "Babies ask their mommies for carnival money. Big kids earn their own income." Juan unzipped his hip bag and held a crumpled wad of cash in his cousin's face. Javier paused, realizing how easy it would be to grab the money and run.

"Whatever," Javier said, ignoring his impulse. "I bet you chickens won't even ride the Scrambler." When no one had a witty response for that, he grinned and ran off with his friend.

Oh no . . . the Scrambler, Skyler thought. She had hoped no one would mention the terrifying ride. Her stomach fluttered and her blood felt electric. *Anxiety*, she thought.

"Hmm," Juan said, returning his focus to the ticket booth. "Rides are between three and five tickets each. Each ticket costs a buck. Or we can get an unlimited-rides wristband for twelve bucks. That means if we are going to go on more than three rides, which we obviously are, we're better off getting the wristband."

Skyler and Izzy took his word for it, and they each bought an unlimited-rides wristband. They felt very grown up spending their own money on such access, but the height of the ticket counter quickly reminded them that they were still kids. They stood on tippy-toes as the lady in the ticket booth helped each of them put on the bright orange wristband. With the paper bracelets almost glowing on their wrists, the kids stepped to the side and surveyed the environment. They felt a sense of power in being able to ride anything they wanted.

"Whoa ... the Scrambler," Izzy said. Following her pointing finger, three sets of eyes looked up and locked on the most fearsome ride of all. High overhead, a dozen caged people spun upside down and swirled side to side. The arm of the Scrambler swung the cage in a giant loop, while the cage spun on its own axis. The screams that hit their ears seemed to wobble, as if the sound itself was flipping and turning. Izzy wiped her sweaty palms on her shorts. Juan gulped. Skyler thought about going home, but she pointed to something more her speed instead.

"Let's start with the bumper boats and then work our way around," she said. The bumper boats did not have a line, so the kids flashed their wristbands and each boarded their own personal boat. Skyler chose purple, Izzy chose blue, and Juan chose orange.

The boats rocked as the kids stepped in. Izzy tried her best to keep smiling when her boat drifted from the dock with only one foot on board. She slowly stretched into the splits and was about to fall into the disgusting water below when a carnival worker with a long stick hooked the boat and brought it back to the dock. Another child, who wasn't with the Grove Street crew, climbed into a yellow boat. When all the kids were safely aboard, the guy with the stick looked around for any stragglers and then pushed a big red button, sending a jolt of power to the boats. The boats jerked forward, and the kids randomly pushed pedals and turned their wheels, trying to figure out how the dang things worked.

Juan immediately drove into a corner, where a bunch of empty boats closed him in.

"Hey," he called out, "there's no reverse on this thing! A little help?"

The stick guy strolled over, snapping his gum and scrolling on his phone. He absentmindedly nudged Juan back into the lagoon, and Juan took off in hot pursuit of Skyler.

Skyler found that if she cranked the steering wheel in one direction and held it in place while pushing the gas pedal all the way down, her boat would spin in circles. After pushing the pedal and shifting the lever near the wheel a few times, Izzy, however, gave up on driving her boat. With her arms folded behind her head and feet kicked up on the front of the boat, she took the opportunity to relax after yesterday's hard work at the lemonade stand. Izzy closed her eyes and a grin spread across her face while she drifted toward Skyler, who spun faster and faster, and who Juan targeted, pedal to the metal.

Juan smacked the purple blur that was Skyler

with more force than the bumper boats had ever known. At that precise moment, Izzy, still kicked back and relaxed, drifted right into Skyler's out-of-control path. This collision, in turn, sent Izzy careening off-kilter toward the edge of the lagoon, where the stick guy crouched, pushing the other kid out of the corner. Izzy scrambled to sit up and put her hands and legs inside the boat, like the announcement had said, but it was too late.

Her foot hooked the stick guy's stick and pulled it—and the stick guy—toward the edge. Things seemed to move in slow motion for a moment as the stick guy managed one big, bug-eyed look before careening down with a fantastic *splash!* The disgusting water of the Mount Brighton carnival bumper boats lagoon rippled as he disappeared underneath. A sudden stillness interrupted the preceding chaos.

"Did you kill him?" Skyler whisper-shouted.

"Me?!" Izzy snapped back. "You're the one who knocked me into him."

"Nuh-uh! Juan rammed me!" Skyler cried.

"What?!" Juan said defensively. "They're called *bumper* boats."

The friends all watched the grayish-greenish water with trepidation. The other kid, still stuck in the corner, yelled for his dad. Then there was a ripple. With a cry, the stick guy punctured the oily film on top of the water and emerged like the Swamp Thing from the lagoon.

Band-Aids and soggy Cheetos clung to his long hair, which wasn't that clean to begin with.

"My *PHONE!*" he bellowed. The kids moved so fast, they couldn't even remember how they got out of the boats. They tore across the carnival and ducked behind the pizza truck, struggling to catch their breath. Finally, a safe distance away, the three friends burst into laughter.

"I've never been so excited and scared at the same time!" Juan said, panting.

"Yeah," Izzy agreed, "this is a whole new emotion for Señorita Flores's mood meter."

"I think this feeling is called exhilaration," Skyler chimed in. She noticed that exhilaration felt the same as anxiety—thumping heart, fluttering tummy, sweating palms—but it somehow seemed exciting instead of scary.

As the kids caught their breath and recounted

what had just happened ("Did you see his face?" "Was that an old sock on his ear?" "How do you lose a sock in the bumper boats lagoon, anyway?"), the comforting aroma of Mr. Lombardi's pizza surrounded them like a hug. Mr. Lombardi owned Chow Bella Pizza, a Mount Brighton favorite because the food was delicious and the restaurant was made with kids in mind.

Mr. Lombardi had a dog named Bella—a Chow Chow whose smooshed-yet-fluffy face, complete with a slice of pepperoni pizza in her mouth, was the logo for the restaurant. There were Chow Chow dogs hidden all over the restaurant, and the paper placemats had a scavenger hunt for kids to find them all. There were also video games, board games, toys to play with, and cartoons playing on a big TV. There was even a make-your-own-pizza station with a kid-height counter and bathroom sinks that you didn't even need a step stool for. You didn't have to dress up to go to Chow Bella; it was a come-as-you-are sort of place, which made it comfortable and fun and like you could just be yourself.

Mr. Lombardi recently invested in a pizza truck so that he could sell Chow Bella pizzas anywhere he parked it. Perched proudly atop the truck stood a larger-than-life fiberglass Bella. Even better, the truck's horn barked instead of beeped. The kids all had the idea to get pizza for lunch at the same time, but before anyone could say it out loud, something stole their attention.

"Of course, I did it!" a voice cried.

"Shh!" Skyler said, tugging Juan and Izzy to crouch behind the truck. They peeked slowly around a dog bone mounted to the hood of the truck, while the fiberglass Bella looked down on them from above.

"Who said that?" Juan whispered.

The voice sounded sinister and calculating, but also familiar. It was coming from the line to the roller coaster, which was across from the pizza truck.

Another voice responded in hushed tones that they couldn't quite hear.

Then the first voice said, "They'll never know! How could they ever find out? I'm glad I did it. I hate cheese. Cheese makes me sick."

"Weird," Juan muttered before Skyler flapped her hands frantically to quiet him down. She needed to hear this.

"They better not be talking about my hamster!" Izzy said, pushing off Skyler's hand to stand and lurch toward the line.

"Izzy, relax!" Skyler whispered quickly. "Cheese is fine. I'm sure we don't even know that kid."

Still, it was hard to ignore the sudden sinking feeling. After all, a good detective never ignores a clue. And what better clue is there than someone confessing to a crime?

"Let's pretend we're going to check out the

roller coaster," Juan suggested. "Then we'll see who it is."

"OK. But we have to be nonchalant," Skyler insisted, glancing side to side.

Izzy and Juan gave her the same bewildered look she'd been getting her whole life—well, at least since she learned to talk.

"It means act casual. Play it cool," Skyler quickly clarified.

Standing stiffly, the three kids wandered over to the roller coaster line, whistling and kicking dirt on the ground, trying not to appear too obvious. Juan got impatient and grabbed a kid by the shoulders and asked her to say "I hate cheese" so that he could try to match the voice.

"That's too chalant, Juan! You have to be *non*chalant," Izzy scolded, pulling him away by his T-shirt sleeve.

"Oh, hey, guys!" said a voice from the front of the line. Juan, Skyler, and Izzy froze and exchanged looks. That was the voice! They slowly turned around to see Declan smiling and waving at them.

Izzy, Juan, and Skyler burst into laughter.

"Oh, it's just *you!*" Izzy said.

"We heard you talking and thought—"Juan started.

"—that you were up to something nefarious!" Skyler finished. "That means evil," she added quickly.

The three friends cracked up, but Declan only managed a forced smile. The color fell from his face, and he wiped his clammy hands on his shorts. "I just remember I have library books to return," he blurted out, quickly running off and leaving his place as next in line for the roller coaster.

His dad chased after him, calling, "But we don't even have a library card!"

"Weird," said Juan.

"Yeah," said Skyler and Izzy together.

Confused but hungry, the kids returned to their original plan of pizza for lunch. Mr. Lombardi said they came just in time—for some reason, he was running low on ingredients.

"I must have left a bag of cheese at the restaurant. It's so unlike me," he said, scratching his head and looking all around the truck.

Izzy got a plain slice, Juan got a pepperoni slice, and Skyler got a white slice that Mr. Lombardi made just for her because he knew she didn't like red sauce.

"The pizza was three bucks a slice," said Juan, his mouth full of gooey cheese and pepperoni, "so that means we each have five bucks left."

"Carnival games are five dollars each!" Izzy exclaimed.

Juan frowned. "Yeah, but those are a rip-off. No one ever wins them—they're totally rigged."

"Face painting is five dollars," Skyler offered.

"Or we could get cotton candy for two dollars and have a little left over," Juan said.

"Why don't we check out the games and see if there are any that aren't rigged?" Izzy suggested, dreaming of winning a giant stuffed animal.

When they arrived at the games area, flashing lights and buzzers overwhelmed their senses, and carnival workers cries of "Step right up for a chance to win big!" competed for their attention. The games looked pretty fun, but the prizes captivated them.

A father and son strolled past, proudly showing off a giant googly-eyed hot dog they had won.

"They're probably plants," Juan remarked cynically. This confused Skyler, because none of the prizes were plants. They were all animals and food and stuff. She scribbled down *other meanings for plant* in her notepad so that she would remember to look it up. Izzy marveled at the stuffed hot dog and wondered how they beat the odds.

The kids meandered through row after row of games, fighting the urge to spend their last five dollars on what they knew was a futile effort. When they turned the corner, they saw a little kid with three giant stuffed animals stacked in her arms. The prizes hid her face, but next to her was a familiar one.

Lucia sat, dart in hand, aiming at a balloon. She had two giant stuffed animals on the ground next to her—one penguin with a goofy face and one rather angry-looking gorilla. It looked like there was a third prize behind the penguin, too.

"Get the unicorn! GET THE UNICORN!" cried the muffled voice next to her, which teetered sideways, about to lose balance under the pile of prizes.

With military-like precision, Lucia launched the dart toward the only remaining balloon.

POP!

"We have a winner," the carnival worker said unenthusiastically. She looked defeated.

"I'll take the unicorn, please," Lucia said victoriously.

"YAY!" exclaimed the other kid, jumping up and down so much that the stack of oversized stuffies tumbled to the ground and revealed the mystery assistant was Phoebe.

"Holy smokes, Lucia! Did you win all of these?!" asked Juan incredulously.

"Yeah," said Lucia smugly, before adding in a humbler tone, "I've had a lot of practice."

"Whoa," said Skyler and Izzy in unison.

"And this is only half of it!" Phoebe interjected, "My dad just left to put the first stash in the car 'cause we couldn't carry them all anymore!"

"You're cleaning us out, kid," the lady in the balloon-pop booth said, handing a majestic pink-and-purple unicorn to Lucia. Lucia nodded in a way that said *That one's for her.* The carnival worker passed the prize to Phoebe, who jumped and squealed with so much excitement that the kids thought she might pass out.

"Do you guys want one?" Lucia asked, turning to the three of them.

"Really?" Skyler gasped. She could not believe such generosity—these were the *grand* prizes.

"Sure! I have a bunch more in Phoebe's car.

And I'm pretty sure I have these ones already from last year. Mi mamá me va a matar si traigo más a casa," Lucia said.

"I doubt she'd actually *kill* you," Juan said.

"I don't know," Lucia said. "Have you seen the look on that gorilla's face? Six more in the house might push her over the edge," she joked.

Izzy picked the goofy-looking penguin, and Juan chose the angry gorilla.

"What's that one?" Skyler asked, pointing to an orange prize behind the penguin.

"I think it's a cheese," Lucia responded, reaching down to pick it up so that they could get a better look. It was, in fact, a neon orange, cross-eyed wedge of cheese that was sticking out its tongue.

"Yes, please!" Skyler cried, hugging the cheese as she snatched it from Lucia. *That's three cheeses so far*, Skyler thought. *The Gorgonzola, the hamster, and now the prize.*

"Did you guys see Declan earlier?" Lucia asked. "He went running past us and was being super weird. I offered him the big cheese, and he stormed off, saying everyone was on his case about cheese today."

"His loss," Skyler said, giving the cheese an affectionate squeeze.

"Oh, we saw him," Izzy said, narrowing her eyes. "And my gut tells me he's up to no good."

"My gut tells me we should get cotton candy," Juan said. So, Skyler, Izzy, Juan, Lucia, and Phoebe went off in search of sugar.

5

CONVERSATIONS

Meanwhile, on carnival day, what Izzy's mom had hoped would be a quiet morning turned into anything but. Just after Izzy left in the morning, there was a knock on the door. Señorita Flores, who also lived in the neighborhood, stopped by to return an air mattress she had borrowed for some out-of-town guests.

"Thanks again for this, Sofia," she said.

"Please, come in!" Izzy's mom replied. She waved the teacher in and offered Señorita Flores some tea. While Izzy's mom prepared the tea in the kitchen, Señorita Flores noticed the hamster cage.

"Oh, how cute! Is it OK if I take a look?" she asked.

"Of course," Izzy's mom called from the kitchen.

Señorita Flores opened the top of the cage

and leaned over to gently stroke Cheese's head. The hamster scurried over to his exercise wheel and began running in place.

"I've been thinking of getting one of these for my Anna. Are they very much work?" she asked.

"No, not really," Sofia replied. "Izzy is doing a great job remembering to make sure he has food and water. I have to stay on her case about cleaning the cage regularly, as you can probably smell, but other than that it's very straightforward and teaching her some good responsibility."

"I cannot stand how cute he is! That settles it then. I'll pop over to Petopia this afternoon. Anna will be so excited!" the teacher said.

"That's where we got Cheese!" Sofia said. "There's a whole litter of them there. Maybe you'll get one of his brothers or sisters. Excuse me a second. I just need to call Izzy home to take care of her chores before they all leave for the carnival." Sofia held the phone to her ear with her chin and shoulder while she filled the kettle at the sink.

Just then, there was another knock on the door. Sofia put the kettle on the stove, lit the burner, and walked to the door while telling her daughter she had to finish her chores before she was allowed to go to the carnival. She swung the door open to see Declan standing on the porch. He muttered something under his breath while Sofia spoke into the phone to Izzy. She nodded to Declan, who tore through the house.

"Hola, Dec—" Señorita Flores began, but he was already out of sight. She jumped when the bathroom door slammed shut. The teacher joined Sofia back in the kitchen. After a quick cup of tea, Señorita Flores started for home. On her way out, she asked, "Do you know the older gentleman who lives on the corner? There was a lot of yelling coming from the window when I walked past. I hope he's OK."

"Mr. Rossi. Yes, I know him a little." Sofia sighed. "I'll go check on him after Izzy finishes her chores. I have something for him anyway, so it's a good excuse to visit. Thanks for letting me know." Just then, Sofia's phone rang. "I'm sorry, I need to take this. It's the plumber—we've got a leak in the basement," she added apologetically.

"Have a great rest of the weekend," Señorita Flores called as she headed down the driveway.

A few moments later, Izzy dramatically stomped in and frantically worked through her to-do list. Her mom was still deep in conversation with the plumber.

"Hang on a second," she said into the phone.

"Izzy, don't use the bathroom. I'm on with the plumber." She sounded frazzled.

Izzy rolled her eyes at her mom, annoyed she would interrupt the best day of the year—the Mount Brighton carnival.

"There, are you happy now?" she said grumpily when she finished her chores. Her mom nodded absentmindedly, and Izzy ran back to Skyler's house, ready to join her friends and spend yesterday's lemonade earnings on a day of fun. Moments after the door slammed behind Izzy, Declan slipped out of the house, undetected.

+ + + + +

As Izzy's mom approached Angelo Rossi's door, a sharp, smoky smell replaced the usual aroma of Bolognese sauce. She had just raised her hand to knock on the door when it suddenly burst open. An irate Mr. Rossi appeared, shaking a fist and screaming at a squirrel on his bird feeder, "Smettila, scoiattolo!"

Smoke wafted out from the kitchen, and seconds later the high-pitched beeping of the smoke detector sent him storming back inside, waving a dish towel angrily at the ceiling to make the alarm stop.

"Smettila, rilevatore di fumo!" he screamed.

Sofia didn't wait for an invitation. She rushed inside and turned off the stove, where a pot billowed black smoke.

"Mr. Rossi, Angelo, are you OK?"

Defeated, the old man plopped himself down at the kitchen table and put his head in his large, worn hands.

"Francesca," he said solemnly, without knowing the English words to say what he meant.

Sofia thought for a moment. Her worried

expression faded to a frown. She remembered that Francesca was Mr. Rossi's late wife. She had passed away over the summer, and the house on the corner had gone dark. The family had always kept to themselves. Their adult son left for college many years ago and never returned, so the older couple had been alone in the small bungalow on the corner. They didn't get out much and didn't engage with the rest of the neighborhood, but the house was alive when Francesca was still there. Warm yellow light from table lamps shone out of the windows, and rich, passionate Italian music would play well into the evening.

Sofia remembered Francesca tending to her rosebushes and sharing a kind smile with neighbors as she meticulously trimmed them. But the most memorable thing Sofia could recall were the aromas that came from the kitchen. Every night a new, savory scent would seep out from the window to the lawn and then onto the sidewalk, making the mouths of whoever walked past water with envy. When Francesca died, the music stopped and the only remaining aroma was Bolognese sauce, night after night.

"Mr. Rossi, tranquilo, tranquilo," Sofia said, rubbing his back reassuringly. "What's all the fuss about?"

The old man launched into an explanation in Italian, but Sofia caught only a few words. She glanced at a handwritten recipe, stained with years of sauce and oil, in what she assumed was Francesca's delicate penmanship.

"Are you trying to make this?" Sofia inquired gently.

"Sì," replied Mr. Rossi, head still in hands.

Sofia tried to read the recipe, but she just

couldn't understand it.

"I know!" she said suddenly, reaching for her purse. She dug out her phone and opened an app. "Izzy showed me this. It's so cool!"

Sofia held the phone above the recipe and Francesca's Italian handwriting transformed to English text on the screen.

"Stupefacente," whispered an astonished Mr. Rossi. He grabbed the phone and wandered the house, holding it over any writing he could find. He marveled at its capacity to change English to Italian, and Italian to English. He pointed it at a Mystery Mayhem flyer Francesca had taped to the fridge the day that Skyler fell in his yard. The phone translated the English text, "Hide a clue and find community," to Italian in bold yellow letters. He studied the screen for a moment, as if trying to decode an elaborate puzzle.

Sofia noticed his unusual scrutiny. "The kids love that game," she said.

Mr. Rossi scrunched up his brow. He didn't understand. Returning his attention to the app he asked, "Cos' è questo?" before jamming his large finger onto a microphone icon on the screen.

"Parlare," the phone instructed in a robotic Italian accent. The old man startled.

"Puoi aiutarmi cucinare?" he spoke into it hesitantly.

"Can you help me with the cooking?" the phone translated aloud.

Sofia looked at Mr. Rossi. Mr. Rossi looked at Sofia. And they both burst into laughter.

After years of living as neighbors, they could finally communicate! They spent an hour trading the phone back and forth, waiting for the robo-voice to translate what the other had said. Sofia learned that Mr. Rossi had not spoken to his son, Matteo, in many years, but he had reached out recently to say he was engaged. Mr. Rossi was to host Matteo and his fiancé on Friday. He wanted to prepare Matteo's favorite family recipe, Casoncelli di Barbariga, and was practicing to get it right. Francesca was the cook in the family, he explained; he only prepared spaghetti Bolognese on Saturdays to give her the night off. Casoncelli di Barbariga was a pasta stuffed with a decadent ham filling, he said. He could make the pasta in his sleep, but the filling just wasn't coming together the way Francesca did it.

His son was angry, Sofia learned, that he and Francesca needed Matteo for everything. Francesca was more outgoing, of course, but the language barrier got in the way. They never learned English and so relied on Matteo anytime they needed to make a doctor appointment or explain something to the plumber. Matteo grew frustrated, he said, because he thought they weren't trying. Mr. Rossi admitted that they didn't try. Matteo was there to translate when they needed it, and there was a community of Italians to socialize with.

Eventually, their friends moved to retirement homes or settled across the country to be with their children who had moved out of state, and the Rossies found themselves alone. The neighborhood was changing, he said. He used to hear equal parts Italian and English on the sidewalk, and then English became more prominent. As the Italian faded, Spanish began creeping in, and today, he lamented, it's all English and Spanish.

There were still many, many Italian families, he explained, but they mostly spoke English now, at least out in public. At the very least, people assumed he was bilingual, and he grew ashamed that he wasn't. He and Francesca used to go downtown to the Italian American Club where familiar words and friendly faces would always greet them. But she was so much more outgoing than Mr. Rossi, and he just didn't feel like he could connect with people the way she could. Sofia thought about her own daughters, Izzy and Olivia, and realized that words, and heritage, and flavors all swirl together to make culture and community.

"What do you say we try this recipe?" Sofia asked. She gently poked the oil-stained recipe card. "And we can practice some English words as we go so that you can impress Matteo."

Mr. Rossi nodded. "Yes," he said, giving English a try.

Sofia handed him a bunch of spinach and a knife. "Spinach," she said.

"Spinaci," he replied. Then, with a small smile, he tried it again: "Spinach."

As the old man began chopping the spinach, Sofia pointed and said, "Chop."

Then she dumped the burned contents of the pot into the trash and picked up a wooden spoon.

"Next time, stir," she said, circling the spoon around the empty pot.

"Stir," he said, mimicking her movement.

"Come si dice prosciutto in inglese?" he asked

her, pointing to the ham on the counter.

"This?" she replied. He nodded. "Ham," she said.

"Ham," he echoed.

The unlikely friends worked through the recipe, exchanging words and smiles as they went. When they were finished, Mr. Rossi packed some of their batch of Casoncelli di Barbariga for Sofia to take home.

"I almost forgot!" Sofia said, reaching into her purse for the triple-bagged Gorgonzola. Its odor somehow managed to escape all three bags.

"Gorgonzola . . . grazie?" the old man said, a little bewildered by the unusual gift.

"This was fun," she said. "Let's practice again soon."

"Sì, sì, grazie," he replied. And they didn't even need the phone to understand each other.

6

DISAPPEARING CHEESE

Meanwhile, Skyler, Izzy, and Juan trudged up the hill behind Skyler's mom, exhausted from the day at the carnival. Izzy hugged her giant penguin in front of her, barely able to see over its head; Juan gave his gorilla a piggyback ride; and Skyler dragged the giant neon orange cheese behind her, wearing a hole in the tip of the wedge as it bumped against the sidewalk.

As they rounded the corner onto Grove Street, Skyler noticed a delicious smell in front of the Zmetila's house . . . a *different* delicious smell. That was not meatball sauce!

"Mmm," Juan said, "someone's having somethin' good tonight!"

The group froze in their tracks, however, when they saw Izzy's mom emerge from the Zmetila's front door. Skyler's heart thumped in her chest as the old man looked up to see the group.

"I should have asked first, but I hope you enjoy cheese!" Izzy's mom joked. She waved goodbye and continued down the front path, still laughing.

"Mom, look for clues!" Izzy yelled between her teeth.

The beacon around Skyler's neck began to beep and glow. The Zmetila locked eyes with her. A chill crept down Skyler's spine. His uncharacteristically jovial expression instantly melted away to reveal his standard grimace. Abruptly, he slammed the door shut. Halfway back to the sidewalk, Izzy's mom jumped.

"What were you doing in there?!" Izzy demanded as her mom joined the group.

"Relax, Izzy. I was just helping him cook, um . . ."—Izzy's mother searched for the name of the Italian dish—"an old family recipe," she concluded, giving up.

"He's creepy, Mom," Izzy said.

"Did you see any Mystery Mayhem clues?" Juan interrupted.

The moms both laughed one of those condescending laughs grown-ups do even when kids aren't trying to make a joke.

"I don't think he plays Mystery Mayhem, kids," Skyler's mom said with that annoying all-knowing parent tone.

Juan's house was right next door to the Zmetila's. As the group shuffled along the sidewalk, they saw Javier sitting crisscross on the porch, organizing some CharmBots cards. When he saw the kids approach with all their prizes, his eyes got bigger than flying saucers.

"Whoa, did you guys win those?!" Javier asked incredulously, running toward the group. "Lemme see!" He snatched the gorilla off his cousin's shoulders and, with a mean grin, punted it high into the sky.

"Hey!" cried Juan. "Give it back!"

"Juan, Javier, take it easy," Skyler's mom said wearily.

"Sorry," Javier said disingenuously. He didn't sound sorry—he still sounded jealous. He jabbed the gorilla's big squishy belly one more time. "Hey, did you guys hear about Declan? He left the carnival in an ambulance. People are saying he got thrown off the Scrambler. The worker was distracted by his phone and forgot to lock the door."

The kids turned to the moms, worried about their friend. Even Javier looked a little concerned.

"I'm sure that's not true. I'll check in with Declan's parents to make sure he's home safe. It sounds like a classic Mount Brighton Elementary School rumor if you ask me," Skyler's mom said reassuringly.

As Skyler's mom texted Declan's dad, Juan and Javier headed inside. Exhausted, the girls and their moms dragged themselves down the street to Izzy's house. She said her goodbyes and tore up the driveway with a sudden burst of new energy, excited to tell Olivia and her dad all about her day.

Skyler and her mom strolled to the end of

Grove Street, holding hands and talking about the carnival. As they turned down the driveway past the end of the street, Skyler felt content, as if everything she needed existed right there on Grove Street.

Suddenly, a piercing scream ripped through the tranquility of the evening as Izzy's voice rang out. "Skyler! Juan! Something terrible has happened!"

Skyler and Juan bolted toward their friend, who was now standing at the end of her driveway in tears. Izzy's mom and Olivia stood in the doorway, looking concerned.

"What happened?" Juan asked between gasps for breath.

"Cheese is GONE!" Izzy wailed.

"Again?" Skyler and Juan asked at the same time, before realizing that their friend needed help.

"Iz, I'm sure Cheese is here somewhere," Izzy's

mom said calmly. She rubbed her daughter's back in soothing circles. "Your friends will help you look. I've got to get dinner started, but I'll join the search just as soon as I can."

"Breathe, Izzy," Skyler said. "You won't be able to find Cheese if you're all worked up."

"The Grove Street Detective Agency is at your service," Juan said.

"Yeah, no one can crack a case like us, Iz," Skyler said, tossing the giant stuffed cheese aside. It landed in a corner of the porch, stuffing springing out of the hole.

"Let's go look for clues!" Juan suggested, trying to brighten the mood.

Inside, Skyler reached into her pocket for her trusty yellow notepad. She wrote *THE CASE OF THE MISSING CHEESE* in bold letters across the top of a blank page. The kids approached Cheese's cage, scouring the surroundings for any clues.

"Did you touch anything?" Juan asked.

"No," Izzy replied. "I didn't even open the cage—I could see he was gone and …" Izzy trailed off, her lip quivering.

"Hmm," Skyler said. She put a finger to her lips, the way she saw detectives do on TV shows when they were thinking hard. "The lid is on tight. There's no way he could get out of there on his own. That leaves two possible scenarios. Either he's still in there, or someone took him."

"He's probably still in there," Juan said dismissively, throwing the lid off. Izzy carefully lifted the plastic log and felt the sawdust on the bottom for any sign of Cheese.

"Nothing. He's gone. Someone *took* him," Izzy lamented.

"Let me check," said Skyler. She put her

notebook on top of a shoebox sitting on a nearby shelf and ran her fingers even deeper in the sawdust. Suddenly her hands stopped. "I think I found something!"

Izzy and Juan crowded around Skyler as she pulled something small and shiny out of the cage.

"What is that?" Izzy asked.

"I think it's a barrette," Juan replied, grabbing the object and blowing off the sawdust.

All at once the kids came to the same realization....

"Señorita Flores," they all whispered.

Skyler grabbed her notepad and scribbled, "Clue 1: Señorita Flores's barrette inside the <u>closed</u> cage!" She underlined the word *closed*.

"Mom, was my teacher here today?" Izzy asked, staring at the barrette in disbelief.

"Just for a little while," replied Izzy's mom, who did not seem to grasp the urgency of the situation.

The kids looked at one another, stunned.

"There must be some other explanation," Juan said, answering the unspoken question. After all, why would Señorita Flores steal a student's pet hamster?

"We need to investigate tomorrow at school,"

Skyler said finally. "Remember, Señorita Flores is innocent until proven guilty. And she can't know we're on to her . . . otherwise we'll never get to the bottom of this."

The real mystery had begun, and their teacher was the one and only suspect.

7

SUSPECT NUMBER ONE: SEÑORITA FLORES

The three friends peeled into Mount Brighton Elementary School, throwing backpacks and jackets in cubbies and huddling behind a bookshelf to make a plan. They were the first kids in school, which basically never happened, and they needed to search for clues before the bell rang.

"You take the teachers' lounge," Juan said to Skyler. "Izzy, hang out in the classroom and listen to all the teacher chatter you can. If she's not in there yet, check her desk for clues. I'll scope out the library—sometimes she goes there before class starts to refill the book cart."

Skyler walked briskly down the hallway, admiring the student work on both walls. On one side, poems about community were written in English, painting a vibrant picture of Mount Brighton. On the other side, blueprints for student inventions were accompanied by Spanish explanations. As Skyler walked past her double-sided toothbrush, *¡Cepillo de Dientes Doble!*, she felt proud of her invention that brushes top and bottom teeth at the same time.

She rounded the corner to the teachers' lounge and suddenly realized she would need to come up with a good excuse as to why she was in that part of the building. There was no reason for a third grader to be lurking outside the teachers' lounge fifteen minutes before school started. As the all-too-familiar fear rolled through her veins, Skyler reminded herself she was here for her friend. Before she could come up with an excuse, however, Skyler froze. She could hear Señorita Flores's sunshiny voice.

"How was your weekend?" asked Mr. Campbell.

"It was pretty good," Skyler heard Señorita Flores reply. "We celebrated Anna's fourth birthday on Saturday. Oh!" The teacher broke off, the excitement apparent in her voice. Skyler crept closer to hear the rest: "And I finally did it!"

"Did what?" asked Mr. Campbell, as Skyler mouthed the same question.

"I got Anna a pet! A hamster. I took one look at Izzy's, and I couldn't resist. I probably shouldn't have, but I did it!" the teacher confessed.

Skyler's face felt hot, and her heart thumped in her chest. She was stunned—frozen to the spot in disbelief.

"Skyler!" said Señorita Flores as she walked out of the lounge, coffee in hand. Skyler jumped. "¿Por qué estás aquí?"

"Um, I, uh, got lost," Skyler stammered unconvincingly.

"Lost?! We've been in school for weeks already! How could you lose your way? Come on, silly, let's get to class. ¡Vámonos!"

When Skyler entered the room with Señorita Flores, her face was still flushed. Juan and Izzy sat at their assigned seats, looking up curiously, but Skyler just shook her head. She was late—every desk was full except hers and Declan's—and with Señorita Flores right behind her, she couldn't say anything to her friends. Until the end of class,

Skyler had a secret. It shook inside her, bursting to get out. A terrible, terrible secret.

+ + + + +

That afternoon, the three kids made sure to get into the lunch line together.

"You guys," Skyler said between her teeth, "I think she did it." The lunch helper scooped a heaping spoonful of rice medley onto her tray.

Izzy turned sheet white and moved through the line stunned, not even responding when asked if she wanted chocolate or vanilla pudding. The kids shuffled to a corner table, too distracted by this news to even think about eating lunch.

In hushed tones, Skyler explained everything she overheard to Juan and Izzy.

"So, she just admitted it to another teacher?!" Izzy asked, incensed.

"She didn't exactly admit to stealing Cheese

specifically," Skyler clarified, "but she did say she *finally did it.*"

"I don't understand," said Juan. "Something's not right. Why would one of our favorite teachers steal a student's pet? Remember Mystery Mayhem Pro Tip Number One: motive is everything."

"She said it was for her daughter's birthday," Skyler offered. "Maybe she didn't have enough money to buy one. My mom always says teachers don't get paid enough."

"I bet hamsters are really expensive," Juan remarked. "I mean they're, like, alive."

"I bet she didn't even have house guests! The air mattress was probably an excuse to break into my house and steal Cheese!" Izzy cheeks transformed from ghost white to fire engine red, and the increase in her volume drew some unwanted attention from the lunch aid. Skyler scribbled *air mattress ruse?* in her notepad and circled it three times.

"We have to confront her," Juan finally declared. "The three of us need to stay after school and tell her we know what she did."

"Maybe she'll give Cheese back," Skyler said comfortingly to her friend. "Señorita Flores is always telling us to give people a chance to make it right. I'm sure she'll return Cheese once she thinks about what she's done."

+ + + + +

The school bell rang and brought with it the chaos of dismissal. As kids ran out of the building, Izzy, Skyler, and Juan stayed glued to their seats. Izzy reached in her pocket and ran her fingers over Señorita Flores's barrette, partly to calm her nerves and partly to remind herself that this was really happening. Her teacher had stolen her hamster.

"Juan, you'd better hurry or they'll leave without you. Perderás el autobús," Señorita Flores said, noticing the stragglers in her classroom.

The three kids were silent. Juan's mouth felt dry, but he finally found the guts to say, "We're not going anywhere. We need to talk to you."

Señorita Flores, who had been busily putting chairs on top of desks so that the custodian could mop the floors, stopped. Realizing the seriousness of the kids' demeanors, she put one chair back on the floor and sat down, facing the kids at their level. "Is everything OK? ¿Qué pasa, amigos?" she asked warmly.

Skyler and Juan looked at Izzy, who finally broke the silence.

"Give him back," she said. Her brows pulled down and her nostrils flared.

Señorita Flores was stunned. "Excuse me?" she

asked more sharply than normal.

"Cheese. Give him back," Izzy repeated.

"¿Disculpe?" she said again, sounding more bewildered than annoyed.

"I heard you in the teachers' lounge," Skyler said nervously, glancing from Izzy's angry expression to her teacher's confused face. "Someone stole Cheese, and I heard you say you did it."

Señorita Flores went silent, trying to process what was happening.

"Cheese is her hamster, Miss. Es su mascota," Juan interjected, trying to help his teacher understand.

Señorita Flores started laughing, returning to her usual, sunny demeanor. "Oh, there has been a misunderstanding, friends. I didn't steal Izzy's hamster. I bought a new one at Petopia!"

"Then why was *this* in his cage?" Izzy asked dramatically, thrusting the incriminating evidence in her teacher's face.

"My barrette!" the teacher exclaimed. "I was wondering what happened to it. I was in your house for a visit, Izzy. It must have fallen off when I was petting Cheese. I'm sorry to hear he's missing, but I didn't take him. And I promise I put the lid on tight when I was done."

"A likely story," Juan muttered underneath his breath.

Seeing that her students were dissatisfied with her explanation, Señorita Flores realized she could put their minds at ease. "I can prove it!" she said, hurrying to her purse.

"You better have an alibi in there," Juan said.

"Mystery Mayhem Pro Tip Number Two," Skyler interjected. "Use evidence to confirm an alibi. That means you need to show us proof you didn't pet-nap Cheese."

Señorita Flores rummaged around in her bag for a moment and produced a crumpled Petopia receipt. She handed it to Izzy.

"Habitat: $24.99, hamster wheel: $6.99, rodent water bottle: $3.76, live hamster: $21," Izzy read aloud.

"Hamsters only cost $21?" Juan asked in

disbelief. "Dang, we could have each bought a hamster instead of going to the carnival. If we didn't give Olivia a tip, that is."

"I'm sorry, Izzy. I didn't take Cheese," Señorita Flores said.

"Back to the drawing board," Juan huffed, "and I'm going to be in big trouble for missing the bus."

"But if you didn't take him, who did?" Izzy asked, still processing this turn of events.

"Declan," Skyler said firmly. "Maybe he *was* talking about your Cheese when we heard him at the carnival. And by the way he was talking, it doesn't sound good."

"One problem with that theory, Skyler," Juan said smugly. "Declan didn't even know Izzy *had* a hamster on Sunday."

Señorita Flores sat down nervously. For a

moment she debated whether to share this information with her students, but the words were already coming out.

"Friends," the teacher said hesitantly. "Declan arrived at Izzy's house while I was there. He was not acting like himself at all. At one point, I went to the kitchen to chat with Izzy's mom. I'm not sure where he was then. He was still there when I left. I thought it was odd he would stay for so long when you kids weren't there. He was acting strangely. He wouldn't even stop to talk to me."

The kids stared at Señorita Flores. They had a new suspect, and it was one of their best friends.

8

SUSPECT NUMBER TWO: DECLAN

The kids decided to go to Juan's house to make a plan. He was supposed to be in robotics club until five o'clock, so they had an empty house and a couple of hours to crack the case before his aunt realized he missed the bus.

They tore down the street, ignoring the beeping beacon as they ran past the house on the corner.

"Let's just take a quick look," Juan pleaded.

"No time, Juan. We need to figure this out," Skyler said without stopping. She knew she wouldn't be able to hold her friends back for long, but with a *real* mystery to solve, she hoped to convince them they didn't have to confront the Zmetila today.

When they arrived at Juan's house, they ran up the creaky wooden stairs and threw their backpacks down in his room. He quickly removed a CharmBots poster from his bulletin board and pinned a fresh sheet of paper to the dark rectangle the sun couldn't fade. On one side he wrote *Señorita Flores*. Skyler jumped up and wrote EXONERATED in big red letters under her name.

"It means she didn't do it," she clarified. On the other side, Juan wrote *Declan*.

"OK, let's think of everything Declan has done

or said over the last few days," Juan said, selecting an orange marker. Skyler started scribbling ideas in her notepad.

"It was odd that he came to my house looking for us. Usually his dad just texts my mom," Izzy said.

"Yeah, and he was super weird when we overheard him after the bumper boats incident," Skyler said.

"He said he wasn't sorry and that he *hated* Cheese," Izzy said, her voice pitching up with outrage. "Do you think Declan *hurt* him?"

"We can't think like that, Iz. Remember, Mystery Mayhem Pro Tip Number Three: we need to stick to the facts," Juan said, trying to bring his friend back from the brink. "Here's a fact: he ran away when we started talking to him. It was super strange."

"And he said he was going to return some library books, but his dad said they didn't even have a library card," Skyler added. "Which is also weird. Who doesn't have a library card?!"

"We need to find out what he did in the library, *if* he even went there," Juan concluded.

"Lucia's abuela works at the library!" Izzy exclaimed. "Let's ask her if she saw anything!"

The kids tore out of the house and headed down the block to Lucia's. They raced up the ramp and hammered on the door. There was no answer.

"Wait! It's Niños y Libros hour at the library," Skyler said, checking her watch. "Lucia's abuela is the storyteller! If we go now, we can catch her before everyone goes home for dinner."

"¡Vámonos!" Juan cried. "Back to the scene of the weirdness!"

The kids cut through yards, climbing over

fences and waving at bewildered neighbors. Their shortcut paid off—they made it just in time. But before they reached the front doors of the library, something froze them in their tracks.

Beep beep beep-beep-beep. The homing beacon sounded, the beeps growing faster and louder as they approached the library. It glowed a warm yellow around Skyler's neck. Juan and Skyler exchanged a look.

"A clue," Juan said, with wonderment in his voice. "That means we only need one more!"

"Forget it, Juan. We don't have time. Cheese is way more important than a silly game," Izzy said.

"There are probably at least three other detective agencies in there, Izzy. If we don't claim the clue now, one of them will snap it up when Niños y Libros is over," Juan pleaded. "*If* they haven't already beaten us to it. *Please* don't let it be a Red

Herring!" Juan crossed his fingers on both hands.

"It should only take a second, Izzy," Skyler said.

Izzy glanced through the library window and saw a group of kids sitting crisscross on the rainbow rug, surrounding Lucia's abuela who expressively read a book. She also saw the iconic Mystery Mayhem beacon hanging around two kids' necks.

"We *are* pretty close to the clue," Izzy said, a little unsure of what to do. She wanted her hamster back more than anything, but she also wanted the Grove Street Detective Agency to crack the case. "I bet we can do both," she resolved. "Let's grab the clue quickly, and then we can get some answers about Cheese. But we need to catch her before she leaves. The more time we waste, the more danger Cheese could be in!"

The kids paced around the entrance to the library, Skyler holding the beacon at arm's length. As she approached the after-hours book-drop bin, the beeping transformed into a single tone and the beacon sparkled with rainbow colors.

"The book drop!" Juan exclaimed.

Izzy ran to the other side of the large, free-standing metal bin, searching for any sign of the Mystery Mayhem clue.

"Nothing!" she said.

Juan stood on tippy-toes and craned his neck to look inside the book chute.

"Nada!" he shouted.

"Nada … nada … nada," the chute echoed back.

Skyler crouched down and felt underneath the book drop, running her hands along the cold metal surface of the bin. Suddenly, she hit a bump. She pulled hard and removed a plastic take-out container that had been affixed to the bottom of the bin with a glued-on magnet.

"Open it!" Izzy cried, looking through the window to see the story-hour kids standing.

From inside the box, Skyler held up a large metal key with a paper tag tied around its ornate handle.

"Congratulations!" Skyler read aloud. "You found the key to solving the mystery. To unlock your next hint, enter code 2675 into your Mystery Mayhem beacon."

She clumsily punched the numbers into the keypad that had appeared on the touch screen. The kids held their breath as people poured out of the library. Would the Grove Street Detective Agency be the first team to find this clue, or would the Red Herring appear on the screen, jeopardizing their chance at becoming the champions? If someone else beat them to it, that annoying red fish meant all that searching was for nothing.

A triumphant trumpet blared from the beacon! The kids jumped with excitement.

Skyler read the text scrolling across the screen: "Impressive work, Grove Street Detective Agency! Only one more clue to crack the case. You'll have to hurry to find it—remember this round of Mayhem has just four days left. Think fast, but don't forget to stop and smell the roses."

"What the heck does that mean?" asked Juan.

"We'll figure that out later," Skyler said, noticing how anxious Izzy was. "Come on."

The kids bolted into the library, dodging the stream of exiting kids and parents.

"She just finished the last book," Lucia said,

approaching her friends. "Did you get the time wrong?"

"No, we came to speak to your grandma," Izzy said. The abuela noticed the kids and walked over with a cheery wave.

"¡Hola, amigos! ¡Juan, te pones mas guapo cada dia!" said the abuela, mussing Juan's hair. He tried to smile politely at the compliment, but he didn't feel particularly handsome, especially not when some old lady was messing up his hair.

"Hola señora, necesitamos su ayuda," Juan replied, backing up to put a little space between him and the overly affectionate grandmother.

Izzy understood the Spanish enough to know that Juan said they needed help.

"Yes!" Izzy added. "Did a boy our age come into the library in a hurry on Sunday? At about one in the afternoon?"

"Sí, sí. He was upset," the old woman replied, frowning slightly.

"Did he return books? Uh, ¿delvolvió unos libros?" Skyler asked, remembering the phrase from the school library.

"No, no. He did not have libros. He ran past and said, 'I hate queso.' He was upset," she replied.

"Oh no!" Izzy lamented. "Queso is Spanish for cheese!"

Juan asked what Declan did in the library in Spanish, and the abuela replied that he went into the bathroom for a long time.

"She said he was in there for like fifteen minutes," Juan said as the kids hurried back to his house, "and that there were lots of flushing noises." The kids looked at one another in silence.

They rounded the corner onto Grove Street, and the beacon went off again.

"We're sooo close!" Juan said, thinking of the Mystery Mayhem clue. "I'm telling you, it's in his yard! We could crack the Case of the Lonely Heart right now! We could win the game!"

Izzy and Skyler exchanged a look. They knew Juan was right.

"Cheese is more important, Juan," Skyler said, biting her lip. It felt like she was stalling, but she couldn't go into that yard. Not now, not ever. "Let's solve the real mystery first, and then if we have time, we can pick up the Mystery Mayhem case."

"You're right," Juan said dejectedly. "Sorry, Izzy. Friends are more important than games."

"Thanks, guys," Izzy said.

Skyler was glad they were doing right by their friend but also relieved that they didn't have to go into the Zmetila's yard. When they got back to Juan's room, he wrote *Did Declan flush Cheese?* in big orange letters on the board.

"Impossible," Skyler said. "Declan wants to be a vet when he grows up. He'd never, ever hurt an animal." They sat in silence, trying to work through the puzzle.

After several minutes, Juan stood up.

"I better go to my aunt's house and fess up to missing the bus before she goes to pick me up," he said with a defeated sigh.

Skyler gathered her things. "Remember, Mystery Mayhem Pro Tip Number One: motive is everything. Let's all keep thinking about Declan's motive," she said. "*Why* would our friend steal Izzy's hamster? And we should think about other suspects, too, so we don't lose time."

Just then, as if on cue, a booming voice thundered through the open window. "ZMETILA!"

Skyler's cheeks went cold.

Izzy shuddered. "He *hates* squirrels."

"Guys," Juan realized, "a hamster is basically a squirrel's cousin." The three friends exchanged a look of fear and curiosity. Skyler wrote *Zmetila* on the paper pinned to the bulletin board, her hand trembling with the terror of the word.

She had thought this real-life mystery was a way to avoid confronting the scary old man on the corner. But now it felt certain: Skyler was going to have to face her fear. And soon. Or Cheese might just stay missing . . . forever.

9

SUSPECT NUMBER THREE: THE ZMETILA

The next day, Izzy and Skyler walked home from school together, discussing theories about Cheese's kidnapping. Juan was at robotics, but the girls couldn't lose any time in their search for answers.

"Declan is definitely our number one suspect," said Skyler. "But we're missing something. Declan is our friend, and he loves animals. I don't think he'd take Cheese, and he definitely wouldn't hurt him."

"He said he hated Cheese multiple times! Even Lucia's abuela heard him say that," Izzy retorted.

"Yeah," Skyler said, trying desperately to reconcile the evidence with what she knew about her friend. Plus, if Declan remained the primary suspect, maybe Izzy and Juan would forget about the Zmetila theory.

"And where is he, anyway?" Izzy asked. "He hasn't been in school all week. His dad probably busted him and he's in big trouble. Maybe his dad even called the police on him. Maybe that's why he's not in school. *'Cause he's in jail.*"

"I think if he were in jail, you'd know, Iz. You are the victim here. You'd probably need to sit for a deposition or something," Skyler said.

"A depowhat?" Izzy asked, annoyed with Skyler's impressive vocabulary.

"It's an interview with lawyers and stuff," Skyler explained.

More confused than satisfied, Izzy continued, "Ask your mom if she ever found out if the Scrambler rumor is true."

"I will when I get home. Right now—" Skyler took a breath—"let's explore the Zmetila theory." She fidgeted with her pencil and nervously bounced her leg. Deep down, Skyler knew her friend wouldn't forget the most fearsome suspect of all, but maybe if she could rule out the Zmetila, they could avoid any interaction with him. "We know he hates squirrels, so he probably hates hamsters, too. But how would he even know you had a hamster?" she asked, biting her lip.

"My mom was at his house that day, remember? She was cooking with him. She said they were using the Translate app to communicate. She probably told him about Cheese!" Izzy said.

"Plus, your mom *was* acting kinda fishy," Skyler said, realizing there may be something to this theory. "Remember? She was being suspicious when you asked what they were cooking. And didn't she say something about Cheese to him as she was leaving?"

Izzy was stunned.

This didn't look good, Skyler thought. The Zmetila might be a legitimate suspect after all.

An idea came to Izzy. "If the Zmetila can communicate with that app, then we could have him sit for a depowhatever."

Skyler's stomach did a flip. She swallowed hard. "Two problems, Izzy. One: we're kids and we don't have phones. And two: no way. He's scary."

"He's a grown-up. All grown-ups have phones," Izzy said. "And there's power in numbers, Skyler. If we do it together, we can find our bravery. I promise we won't leave you alone again."

Skyler studied her best friend. She wouldn't face the Zmetila for a silly game, but for a real mystery? For Cheese? For Izzy? She knew she had to, but the thought made her legs feel wobbly. The girls decided to wait until Juan got home from robotics to fill him in on the plan.

+ + + + +

After dinner that evening, Juan, Izzy, and Skyler walked nervously up the Zmetila's path. It was strange being in his yard—only Skyler had ever seen it from this perspective. It was the kind of house you skip when trick-or-treating. As they approached the house, the beacon began to beep and glow. It grew louder and louder as they approached the steps but softened again when they were on the porch. The kids' eyes darted around, looking for any sign of the Mystery Mayhem clue. Skyler buried the beacon in her pocket to muffle the sound.

"We're here for Cheese, remember?" she reminded her friends. She wanted to get this over with and get out of there as quickly as possible. When they got to the door, the familiar aroma of meatball sauce filled the air.

Izzy drew in a deep breath, nodded at her friends, and found the guts to knock. There was no response.

"He's in there. Why isn't he answering?" Juan asked impatiently.

"'Cause he knows we're on to him!" Izzy declared, with injustice fueling her courage.

"OK, we tried. Let's go," Skyler said quickly, turning around.

"Wait. He's old. Old people walk slower," Juan said, blocking Skyler from the steps.

A few moments later, sure enough, the door slowly creaked open. The Zmetila peered out of the crack, confused that he didn't see anyone, before looking down and realizing that his uninvited guests were short.

"Buonasera," the old man grunted, raising an eyebrow.

"Where's Cheese?!" Izzy demanded, shoving forward like she could force her way through the door.

"Scusami?" the Zmetila responded. His eyes narrowed.

"Izzy, he doesn't understand. We need the app," Juan interrupted. "DO YOU HAVE A PHONE?!" Juan asked slowly and loudly. He suddenly realized that he hated it when people talked to his parents that way, and he felt a little ashamed for doing it.

Skyler pretended to hold a phone to her ear and made a ringing sound. Her palms sweated—she did not like inviting attention from the mean old man, but she had to help her friend.

The Zmetila locked Skyler in a hard stare and did not move his eyes from her as he responded. Finally, he huffed out a breath.

"Un telefono? Sì. Venite." The Zmetila lumbered down the hall. When the kids stayed on his porch, frozen, he turned and gestured for them to follow him inside. The kids took a deep breath and crossed the threshold into the unknown.

Everything was different in the Zmetila's house. It was old-fashioned and dark, and none of the writing on books or notepads made sense in English or Spanish. The Zmetila led them to the kitchen, where a pot simmered on the stove. *Mmm, meatball sauce,* Skyler couldn't help but think. The difference between the fear in her tummy and the delicious-smelling sauce confused her.

He pointed to the wall, where an old rotary telephone hung. The kids had heard of these. They could only be used for calling people—not games, or apps, or texting, just . . . talking. And you couldn't walk around with them because they were tethered to the wall with cords. They didn't even have screens!

"Telefono," the Zmetila grunted.

"No, no," Izzy said. "A cellphone. Like for the internet."

Internet. Mr. Rossi knew that word. "No, niente cellulare," he said, disappointing the kids.

Skyler turned to leave. She grabbed Izzy's wrist, but her friend wouldn't budge. Izzy's eyes welled with tears, and she breathed out a shaky breath.

"We'll have to try to depose him without the translation app," Skyler said, surprised by her own courage.

"I got this," Juan said confidently. "DID-YOU-TAKE-HER-HAM-STER." He was doing it again—speaking that way that hurt his dad's feelings.

The Zmetila's eyes widened and darted side to side as he worked hard to search for words, as if they were still hanging in the air.

"Ah! Si!" he said, brightening. "Ham! Stir!"

"So, you admit it!" Izzy said. "Where is he?!" She stomped her foot, defiantly standing up to the Zmetila.

The old man looked confused and overwhelmed.

Juan realized that if "sí" and "no" were the same in Spanish and the Zmetila's language, maybe there were other similarities, too.

Mystery Mayhem Pro Tip Number One: motive is everything, thought Juan. "Hamster," he said, "¿por qué?" Por qué means why in Spanish and is pronounced "por-kay." In Italian, the word for "why" is perché, which is pronounced "per-kay." It's wasn't the same, but it was close. Mr. Rossi understood.

"Perché ham stir?" Mr. Rossi echoed back. He waved his hands dismissively and began to walk away, overwhelmed with the energy it would take to try to respond. Suddenly, he realized that this was exactly what his son had always complained about. Although these little kids were struggling with his language, they were making an effort. He, on the other hand, wouldn't even attempt to stumble through the English. And that was the poor girl he scolded when Francesca was sick and his emotions got the better of him. Maybe if he tried, the girl would know he wasn't unkind. Maybe she would stop being so frightened by him. He steadied himself. He knew "ham" and "stir"

from his impromptu cooking lesson. It might be clumsy, but he could string together a response in English if he put his mind to it.

The old man took a deep breath. "Why ham stir? I cooked it. To eat," he said, flashing a nervous grin. There was a heavy silence as the kids registered what they had heard.

"AAAAAHHHHHHH!" the three friends screamed and bolted out of the Zmetila's house in terror.

10

EXONERATION

The kids tore into Izzy's house, screaming, trembling, and trying to make sense of what just happened. Juan slammed the front door and immediately turned the bolt.

"Kids, kids, slow down," Izzy's dad said. "What's going on?"

"The Zmetila cooked Cheese! Dad, he's going to eat him!" Izzy wailed.

"The who? Did what?" Izzy's mom interjected, trying to assess the situation.

"The old man on the corner. He cooked your hamster!" Juan said.

"What? Why would Mr. Rossi cook Cheese, honey? I think there's been a misunderstanding," Izzy's mom replied.

"Mom, he admitted it. He said, 'I cooked the hamster to eat it!'" Izzy stopped suddenly. A realization hit her like a bolt of lightning. "Mom! You *knew!* You said you were cooking with him, and you were super weird that night when we asked you what you were doing." Izzy clung to her dad, betrayed by her own mother.

"Oh my gosh, you said you hoped he liked *Cheese* when you were leaving!" Skyler cried, stunned that Izzy's mom was in on the awful crime.

"Is it 'cause she didn't clean the cage? That's harsh," Juan said.

"I didn't cook your hamster, Izzy! Mr. Rossi didn't cook your hamster—no one cooked Cheese! Mr. Rossi doesn't speak much English, kids. I'm proud of him for trying, but he seems to have given you a fright. I'm sure he's shaken up, too. Try not to think about it tonight. We'll all go over there tomorrow after dinner. I'll use the translator, and we'll get to the bottom of this."

The kids would need a strong alibi to clear the Zmetila and Izzy's mom. Mistrust loomed over Grove Street that night—the kids didn't know who they could believe.

+ + + + +

After dinner the next day, the three friends cowered behind Izzy's mom as she knocked on the door. The Mystery Mayhem beacon predictably went off just before the steps to the porch and was still beeping when the somewhat rattled old man answered the door a few minutes later. He gestured for them all to come in and motioned for them to take a seat in the living room.

Sofia opened the app and spoke into her phone.

"Angelo," she said, "these children seem to think you've cooked Izzy's pet hamster." The robotic voice spoke the sentence aloud in Italian. There was a long pause. Then he burst into laughter, tears welling up in his eyes.

"It's not funny!" Izzy said, fighting back her own tears. "He was my pet!"

When he composed himself, Mr. Rossi grabbed the phone and spoke into it. A moment later, the robotic voice said, "That's what I get for trying to speak English. I didn't cook your hamster!" Hearing the app say "hamster" sent the old man reeling again. When he caught his breath, he said "prosciutto" into the app.

"Ham," the app announced.

Then he said, "Mescolare."

"Stir," the app reported obediently.

The information hung in the air for a moment before the kids and Izzy's mom realized what had happened. The room erupted with laughter. Even Skyler couldn't contain a giggle, although she still wanted to get out of there as quickly as possible. When things finally settled, Izzy realized they were no closer to finding her beloved pet.

"So, it must be Declan then," Izzy said.

"Declan? Honey, why would Declan take your hamster?" Izzy's mom replied.

"We have evidence," Juan said. "He came to your house the day Cheese went missing. He was acting weird at the carnival."

"Yeah, we heard him say he wasn't sorry and that he *hated* Cheese," Skyler chimed in.

"And Lucia's abuela said he ran into the library, still talking about how much he hated Cheese and then went into the bathroom for a looong time and made a bunch of flushing sounds," Izzy concluded.

"Oh dear," Izzy's mom said. "Declan didn't take Cheese, kids. Declan was going to tell you this himself at school on Monday, but I think it's important you know the truth so you don't falsely accuse your friend. He's embarrassed, and I'm trusting you to be kind with this information." She took a deep breath. "Declan is lactose intolerant. That means anything with milk can make him sick.

"Before the carnival, his dad took him to Claudia's for a bite to eat. He ordered an arepa. He didn't realize it was filled with cheese. His stomach started to hurt on the way to the carnival. That's why he stopped to use our bathroom. His dad said that when they got to the carnival, Mr. Lombardi was loading supplies into the pizza truck. Declan was so upset that his tummy ache would ruin his favorite day of the year that he dumped a whole bag of Mr. Lombardi's pizza cheese into the trash when no one was watching. His dad saw him and was very disappointed. You must have overheard him getting in trouble."

The kids were silent.

"That explains why he rushed to the bathroom in the library," Skyler said.

"And why he flushed so much," Juan said, realizing what a tummy ache led to.

Izzy's mom continued, "His dad lost sight of him after he ran off. After Declan came out of the library, he was doubled over in pain. A concerned carnival worker called an ambulance. He's going to be fine, and he even got special medicine to take if he accidentally has cheese or milk again. It's just his pride that's a little bruised. And he's very sad he missed the fun of the carnival."

"Poor Declan," said Izzy. "The carnival is his favorite day of the whole year."

"Yeah," said Juan. "People can keep thinking he got thrown off the Scrambler. No one needs to know he really had the cheese poops." The group stared at Juan. "What?!" he asked defensively.

"Mom, maybe we can have Declan over this weekend," Izzy suggested.

"Yeah," Juan said, "there's no school on Friday! We could set up our own carnival. Lucia can be in charge of the games. She knows them better than anyone!"

"We can re-create the carnival for Declan!" Skyler cheered.

Mr. Rossi, who had found an old pair of headphones and had attached them to the phone, had been listening to the story about Declan, translated into robotic Italian. He was touched by the kids' kind ideas.

"I hope you find your hamster," he said to Izzy in perfect English as he walked his guests to the door. He looked at Skyler, searching for the words to appologize for frightening her all those months ago, but all Skyler saw was a grimmacing old man staring her down. Her hair stood on end and she ran down the gravel path, ignoring the beacon as it alerted her to the winning clue.

11

SUSPECT NUMBER FOUR: SKYLER

The three kids walked to school a little slower the next morning, their bodies dragging from the weight of the unsolved mysteries. They were out of suspects and still hadn't cracked the Case of the Missing Cheese, and the only remaining Mystery Mayhem clue for the Case of the Lonely Heart might as well have been at the bottom of a swimming pool full of venomous snakes as far as

Skyler was concerned. Even though the Zmetila didn't cook Cheese, she still didn't want anything to do with him.

"Let's all think of exactly what happened that day, up until we realized Cheese was gone," Skyler said as they shuffled to school.

Izzy recounted watching cartoons with Olivia before setting up the lemonade stand. Juan recalled helping his mom bake brownies. Skyler fessed up that she didn't muddle the pineapple juice, and there wasn't a blue moon. She explained the Gorgonzola situation but confirmed she did still enchant the juice.

"Do you remember the spell, Skyler?" Juan asked.

"I think so. *Pineapple juice, so nice and sweet, bring fortune to the kids of Grove Street,*" Skyler recited.

"That part definitely worked," Juan interrupted, fondly remembering the fortune they made at the lemonade stand and the giant carnival prizes.

"There was more," Skyler continued. "*One more thing to make me cheer, make....*" Skyler froze, realizing what she had done.

"Make what?" Izzy asked, noticing her friend's sudden shift in mood.

"Never mind. It was stupid. Spells are just pretend anyway," Skyler said quickly.

"Tell us," Juan insisted, now picking up that Skyler was holding back.

"*One more thing to make me cheer, make the stinky cheese disappear?*" Skyler said sheepishly.

The friends were stunned.

"How could you?!" Izzy wailed, bolting toward school. Juan chased after her.

"Way to go, Skyler," he called back.

+ + + + +

Skyler was too distracted for word wall or number corner that morning. She kept replaying the spell in her head. Had she really done it?

At lunch, she tried to sit with her friends, but Juan threw his sweatshirt on the open seat and said it was taken.

"I meant the Gorgonzola, you guys," she insisted. "I didn't mean your hamster. I love Cheese."

Still, Izzy and Juan ignored her.

Skyler walked home from school alone that afternoon. She paused in front of the Zmetila's house to study the yard that made the beacon go off. Her heart thumped, but she stood with the feeling, scanning the tidy lawn for any signs of the clue. She made herself stay in front of the house for as long as she could, but when she saw the old man's silhouette in the window, she hurried off down the street. When she approached Izzy's house, she saw the front door slam closed. Izzy had walked fifty steps ahead of her the whole way home and refused to talk to her.

As she passed Izzy's house, Skyler saw the giant cheese prize Lucia had given her on Izzy's porch. She must have left it there in the confusion of that evening. She decided if Izzy was no longer her friend, she should get the cheese now so she didn't have to deal with it later. As Skyler climbed the stairs to Izzy's porch, the door swung open.

Izzy stood with red eyes, wanting desperately for this

latest revelation to be untrue.

"Tell me one more time what you said," Izzy sniffed.

Skyler took a breath and recited, "*Pineapple juice, so nice and sweet, bring fortune to the kids of Grove Street. And one more thing to make me cheer, make the stinky cheese disappear.*' I said *stinky* cheese, Iz. I was talking about the Gorgonzola. Your hamster isn't stinky."

"Yeah, but his cage was until I cleaned—" Izzy stopped short. "Oh no," she said, suddenly realizing what had happened. Izzy crumpled to the floor and held her head in her hands.

"What is it, Izzy?" Skyler asked, embracing her balled-up friend.

"I'm so sorry, Skyler. You didn't make Cheese disappear. I did," she said. "I put him in a shoebox while I cleaned his cage. I was in such a hurry to get to the carnival, I don't think I ever put him back. How could I be so stupid?!" Izzy's voice quivered.

"Izzy, that's great news!" Skyler cheered. "He's probably still in the shoebox, just a little hungry and thirsty."

"Actually, the vet told me to put food and water in the shoebox to make him less scared while I cleaned out the cage," Izzy said, brightening. "He should be OK!"

The girls ran inside. The shoebox was still on the bookshelf, and the lid was still securely in place. Izzy scooped it up and immediately her face fell. Her fingers landed on the far end of the box, where a hole had been chewed through the side! Cheese had escaped. Izzy curled up on the couch.

Skyler took a deep breath. If they couldn't solve the Case of the Missing Cheese, then she knew she had to face her fears and solve the Case of the Lonely Heart. Winning Mystery Mayhem might be the only way to cheer up her friend.

12

CASE CLOSED

It was Friday again, and it had been a week since Cheese escaped. There was still no sign of the hamster. The deadline to crack the Case of the Lonely Heart was at four o'clock, and only one clue stood in the way. Mr. Rossi had been preparing all week for his son Matteo's visit that evening. Matteo was bringing his fiancé, Mia, to meet his father and make amends. Mr. Rossi had been practicing the recipe and English all week, determined to impress his son. He wouldn't be able to say much to Mia yet, but he had practiced "Welcome to the family" and "I'm so glad you're here" over and over again. He carefully prepared the Casoncelli di Barbariga. The filling bubbled on the stove, and it tasted just like Francesca used to make it. He fondly remembered that his wife would always open a window so that the delicious aroma would make the neighborhood jealous. He chuckled to himself as he did the same.

It was a beautiful afternoon, and Juan and Javier played CharmBots on the porch. Skyler ran down the street, collecting Izzy along the way. She had a new sturdiness about her—like she was confident and in charge. She pulled her friend by the arm to Juan's driveway.

"Juan!" Skyler called. "I'm ready. We still have time. We can do this!"

The beacon began to chirp and glow softly.

Juan dropped his CharmBots cards and ran to meet his friends.

"Hey!" Javier protested as Juan ran down the driveway. "I was winning!"

The Grove Street Detective Agency stood, shoulder to shoulder.

"'Don't forget to stop and smell the roses,'" Skyler said, reciting their final Mystery Mayhem hint aloud. They had half an hour left to crack the case, and if they did, they'd be the first kids from Mount Brighton to ever win Mystery Mayhem.

"The roses!" Skyler shouted. "Mr. Rossi has rosebushes in front of his house! The beacon keeps telling us to go there. It went nuts when we knocked on his door. It's time. I'm ready." A new sensation came over Skyler. Her stomach flipped, but instead of running from her fears, she was ready to face them. Bravery didn't feel like not being afraid. No, bravery felt like being afraid and deciding to keep going anyway. Bravery felt like there was something more important than the fear—her friends.

"He's not so bad," she said, mostly convincing herself. "He bought enchanted pineapple juice, he was going to let us use his phone when he thought we needed one, and he even laughed when he figured out the whole ham-stir miscommunication."

"If the final clue *is* in his rosebushes, it's probably just stuck in the branches or something," Juan said.

"Yeah, it'll be super easy to find. He won't even know we're there," Izzy agreed.

"And we're here with you, Skyler. We won't leave you stranded again," Juan said.

"Grove Street Detective Agency, let's do this!" Skyler exclaimed, putting her hand in the center of the huddle of friends. Juan and Izzy did the same.

"¡Vámonos!" they all shouted, throwing their hands in the air.

As the kids approached Mr. Rossi's yard, Skyler got a pit in her stomach, just like always. She thought about turning around, but the beeps grew louder and louder. Juan grabbed her sweaty right hand. Izzy grabbed her left. The three kids took a synchronized step onto the old man's manicured front lawn.

When they reached the rosebushes planted on either side of Mr. Rossi's front steps, the beautiful floral aroma took them off guard. Izzy bent down to smell a rose.

Hearing the beacon, Mr. Rossi peered out the kitchen window and noticed the intruders. He was about to chase them away when he saw all three kids admiring his wife's beautiful flowers. *No harm in that,* he thought, smiling to himself.

Juan then jammed both hands into a rosebush, carelessly feeling around and shaking the delicate plant.

"Yowch!" he cried. "These things are sharp!"

"Duh, those are thorns," Izzy said, thrusting her own arms into a bush and then pulling them out with a wince.

Skyler dropped to her knees and began feeling the dirt under the bushes. The beacon's beeps smoothed to a solid tone and the rainbow lights sparkled.

"It's gotta be burri—" she began.

"SMETTILA!" a powerful voice thundered as

the front door swung open. Juan and Izzy bolted toward the street but stopped before they reached the sidewalk. Skyler jumped to her feet, her eyes darting between her friends and the angry old man in front of her. She dusted herself off, just as she had months ago when he had screamed at her for falling with the Mystery Mayhem flyers.

Her heart fluttered with nerves, but her feet stayed glued to the earth.

The old man lolloped down the steps, angrily chastising her in words she didn't understand.

"Stop it!" Skyler said, surprised at her own bravery. "We were just playing."

The old man took a breath to calm himself, searching for the words to understand Skyler.

"The beacon said to 'stop and smell the roses,'" she sniffed, trying to explain that they weren't bad kids.

Izzy and Juan crept forward, feeling guilty for almost abandoning their friend again.

"Rosa," the old man said, as if he was solving a riddle. "Rosa!" he exclaimed, shuffling inside as fast as he could.

"What is *happening?*" Juan asked between his teeth. The old man's sudden change of mood was unusual.

A moment later, Mr. Rossi appeared holding a piece of paper. Written in his wife's delicate penmanship was *Le rose mi hanno reso felice. Ora è il tuo turno.* The kids crowded around to read the note.

"Some of the words look like Spanish," Juan observed.

"Like *rose* is close to *rosa*," he pointed out.

"And *rose* is *rose* in English," Skyler observed.

"And *felice* sounds like *feliz* in *español*," Izzy chimed in.

"That means 'happiness,'" Skyler finished.

"*Ora è il tuo turno*," the old man breathed. His face relaxed into a mix of happy and sad. *Bittersweet*, Skyler thought.

"That sounds like *ahora es tu turno*," Juan said, translating the phrase to Spanish.

"'The roses brought me happiness. Now it's your turn,'" Skyler said, solving the puzzle and looking up at the large old man with understanding eyes.

Mr. Rossi reached out and grabbed the beacon that hung around Skyler's neck, studying the glowing alarm.

"A-ha!" he exclaimed, turning over the note. The other side featured an image of the same device. Francesca's note was written on the back of one of the Mystery Mayhem flyers Skyler had dropped in the yard. Mr. Rossi looked at the beacon and back at the flyer, realizing they were one and the same.

"'Hide a clue and find community,'" the old man read the front of the flyer aloud. "Francesca!" He laughed, running to his gardening shed.

Skyler looked at her watch. "We have ten minutes left!" she shouted. "Hurry, Mr. Rossi!"

The old man hurried back with a rusty metal shovel. He plunged it into the earth, and it stopped with a sudden clang.

The kids dropped to their knees, scooping out the rich soil at the base of the bush. Mr. Rossi continued digging, doing his best to avoid the frantic little fingers below.

When the old biscotti tin was revealed, eight hands worked together to delicately remove it from the earth.

Skyler tore off the lid.

Inside, a beautifully crocheted yellow heart seemed to glow under the warmth of the afternoon sun. A small label containing the Mystery Mayhem code was pinned to it. "We need to enter the code!" Skyler called out.

"5683!" Juan blurted as Skyler punched the numbers into the beacon.

A fanfare erupted from the beacon, and digital confetti covered the screen.

"'Congratulations, Grove Street Detective

Agency! You are the regional Mystery Mayhem champions! Your grand prize is in the mail! From, your friends at Mystery Mayhem HQ,'" Skyler read from the screen.

The kids cheered, jumping and high-fiving one another. Even Mr. Rossi gave celebratory back pats.

"We did it!" Skyler exclaimed. She turned to Mr. Rossi. "Thank you," she said earnestly.

By now, both of the boys' mothers appeared outside to see what was going on. They joined Javier in peering over the hedge that separated the houses. Mr. Rossi gestured them over to his yard. Juan explained everything in Spanish, and the women laughed in amazement at the kids' victory.

"I guess I was wrong," Javier said sheepishly. "Champions . . . wow! I wonder what the grand prize is!"

Izzy's mom turned the car down Grove Street, returning from the grocery store. She parked and hurried over to join the celebration. Suddenly, a piercing alarm disrupted the conversation. The kids examined the beacon to see if another message from HQ was coming through, but the smell of something burning quickly drew the group's attention to Mr. Rossi's open window. Thick, black smoke billowed out of it.

"No, no, no!" wailed Mr. Rossi, lumbering back to the kitchen. A few minutes later, he emerged, defeated.

Izzy's mom handed him her phone. Using the translator app, he said that dinner was burned, there was not enough time to start over, and his house smelled like smoke. Matteo and Mia would be there in two hours, and the evening was already a failure.

Skyler got that awful feeling again—like she had ruined everything. She braced herself for the scolding Mr. Rossi would surely give her. If it wasn't for the kids and their game, he never would have burned the dinner.

"It's OK," Mr. Rossi said, without the app. He gave her a reassuring look.

Skyler exhaled.

The boys' mothers had a brief exchange in Spanish. Then Javier's mom grabbed the phone, changed the input language on the app, and said, "I'm making tostadas for dinner. There will be plenty!"

Izzy's mom had an idea. "Yes! We'll host a potluck. Matteo and Mia will see how many friends you have made. My house at six. I'll spread the word."

+ + + + +

Skyler and her parents arrived. Her dad added barbecue ribs to the spread of tostadas, pozole, satay chicken, and potato salad. Lucia, Izzy, Juan, and Javier had re-created the balloon pop wall, ring toss, and the guess-which-cup-the-penny-is-under carnival games. Lucia brought several of her giant prizes, which she hung over the side of the porch for winners to peruse. The kids collected old Big Wheels and ride-on toys from various garages and lined them up at the top of the gentle slope in Izzy's backyard.

"It's just like the roller coaster!" Juan declared.

"Great! Now let's get to work on the Scrambler," Javier teased. The kids laughed. Phoebe dashed up the driveway wearing a purple tutu and carrying a big plate of pierogies her grandmother had made. Then Declan's car arrived. His eyes widened as he took in the sight. "It's just like the carnival!" he said, hugging his friends.

Mr. Rossi arrived moments later, dressed in a crisp gray suit with a floral tie. The kids had never seen him so dressed up. Realizing he came empty-handed, he hurried home and returned a few moments later with the Gorgonzola—the only thing he could find to bring. Skyler pinched her nose.

"Why is that the one cheese that keeps coming back?" Skyler asked Izzy, tossing a ring toward an empty soda bottle. "Have you seen your hamster at all?"

"No," said Izzy disappointedly. "I guess I wasn't ready for a pet after all."

"I researched it, Iz. Lost hamsters usually hide in the wall or make nests in soft spaces. He's probably OK," Skyler said, trying to comfort her friend.

Just then a car pulled up and a young man

stepped out. He looked like Mr. Rossi but younger and more optimistic. Matteo opened the door for his fiancé and helped her out. Mia looked nervous.

"Dad?" Matteo called, confused as to why his father was sitting at a table in the neighbor's yard.

"Matteo," Mr. Rossi gasped, rising to greet his son. His eyes welled with tears as his son hugged him tightly. Then he looked at Mia. "Welcome to the family," he said, nervous about his pronunciation. A smile spread across Matteo's face.

"Thank you," Mia replied, equally nervously. "I'm sorry. I only speak a little English."

"We met in a language exchange program. I want to learn Spanish, and Mia wants to learn English," Matteo explained to the surrounding neighbors.

"¡¿Habla español?!" many excited voices interrupted, jumping up and down. Mia was confused and delighted to see so many kids speaking her language with various levels of fluency. When she saw the Guatemalan food and the strangers who somehow looked familiar, she felt a sense of belonging.

"Did you arrange all this?" an astonished Matteo asked his father. "How did you know?"

Mr. Rossi shook his head and laughed. Then he led a round of introductions while the neighborhood chatted. "I almost forgot," Matteo said. He ran to his car and returned with a plastic container of Casoncelli di Barbariga. He added it to the table. "Just like Mom used to make. I practiced for weeks." A happy heaviness lingered between the father and son. "Dad, you're so dressed up!" Matteo teased, giving his father a playful punch on the arm.

"There's just one thing missing," Skyler said.

She reached into her pocket and pulled out the yellow crocheted heart Francesca had made—the winning Mystery Mayhem clue. Using the safety pin that affixed it to the clue card, Skyler pinned the heart to Mr. Rossi's lapel. "There," she said contentedly.

The old man put his hand on Skyler's shoulders and turned to admire the table full of food and yard full of friends. He realized he needed to add his contribution. As Mr. Rossi began to take the Gorgonzola out of its multiple bags, the neighbors backed up.

"Ooof!" Izzy's mom exclaimed when the pungent smell whacked her in the face. "Why don't we keep this one over here?" She put the stinky cheese on a paper plate and moved it to a table on the porch, next to the neon orange carnival prize Skyler kept forgetting. "Skyler, please bring this thing home tonight," she said. "I bet it has squirrels living in it."

Mr. Rossi narrowed his eyes and muttered, "Smettila, scoiattolo."

"Mr. Rossi, what does that mean?" Skyler asked.

Smettila? Mr. Rossi thought, trying to find the word in English.

"It means 'stop it,'" Matteo offered. The kids processed this discovery, feeling like they had solved a somewhat underwhelming mystery.

Skyler climbed the porch stairs to get her carnival prize and put it somewhere she would remember it. Suddenly, something caught her attention. From the hole in the bottom of the cheese wedge, a small pink nose emerged, wiggling between bits of stuffing. The pungent Gorgonzola seemed to capture the nose's attention. It moved forward and was followed by a fluffy brown and white head. Skyler watched for a moment to confirm her eyes were not misleading her.

"Izzy!" she exclaimed. "I found Cheese!" The hamster scurried across the porch and scampered up the leg of the table. It ascended the mountain of Gorgonzola and triumphantly feasted on the stinky cheese.

Izzy held her nose, dashed up the stairs, and grabbed Cheese with her free hand.

"The Case of the Missing Cheese is officially closed!" Skyler declared, raising both fists in the air. The cheers that followed were not English cheers, or Spanish cheers, or Italian cheers, but cheers of joy and friendship. They were Grove Street cheers, and the kids felt lucky to live in such a special place.

THE END

EPILOGUE

Later that evening, after the excitement faded, a cheery orange station wagon drove slowly down the street. A young woman dressed professionally yet fashionably stepped out and gave an enthusiastic wave to the gathered neighbors.

"Hi!" she said. "¡Buenos noches! I'm the new realtor selling the blue house. This looks like a wonderful neighborhood."

"That house is for sale?" Matteo asked. "Mind if we take a look?"

LISA C. MITCHELL lives in a multilingual community with her daughter, husband, and two dogs. Wait a second. That sounds a lot like this book. Huh. She also works in the creative sector and has a doctorate in education. Lisa has written a bunch of stuff, but this is her first children's novel.

Learn more at LisaCMitchell.com

www.ingramcontent.com/pod-product-compliance
Lightning Source LLC
LaVergne TN
LVHW010325070526
838199LV00065B/5651